Sacred Heart Orphanage

The Haunted Series

Book 5

Patrick Logan

Books by Patrick Logan

The Haunted Series
Book 1: Shallow Graves
Book 2: The Seventh Ward
Book 3: Seaforth Prison
Book 4: Scarsdale Crematorium
Book 5: Sacred Heart Orphanage
Book 6: Shores of the Marrow

Insatiable Series
Book 1: Skin
Book 2: Crackers
Book 3: Flesh
Book 4: Parasite
Book 5: Stitches (Spring 2017)

Family Values Trilogy
Witch (Prequel)
Mother
Father
Daughter (Spring 2017)

Short Stories
System Update

Prologue

THIRTY-ONE YEARS AGO

THE NINETEEN CHILDREN, RANGING in age from three to the eldest in his mid-teens, sat patiently at their desks. They were an eclectic collection of individuals, representing all classes and creeds.

But despite their differences, they all had two things in common: they were all orphans and one of their parents had been a Guardian

That is, until Leland murdered them.

The woman at the head of the class was stern and adroit, leaning hard on the children regardless of their age or background, working them harder with every lesson. She was not a mean person, not in the least, but there was no time for coddling; she was well aware of the severity of what they were dealing with, with the responsibility these young boys and girls—mostly boys—were destined to be bestowed with. Although it hadn't been her idea to set up the orphanage, and even though she had initially resisted, the more she taught these children, the more it made sense to her.

After all, the number of Guardians left in this world was perilously low; not all of them had acquired Sean's particular tenacity for survival, his ability to withstand aging.

And the few that remained were being hunted.

The woman raised her head and looked out at the nineteen children, the cherubic faces more colorful than every shade that existed in the long-abandoned Sacred Heart Orphanage.

Not all of them would become Guardians, that much was certain, despite the uncertainty of virtually everything they did at Sacred Heart. Some would grow frustrated, or worse, bored, and leave the orphanage when they turned sixteen. There was nothing that the woman could do to stop them, and even if she could have, she would have resisted the urge. The last thing they wanted to do was train a Guardian that wasn't fully vetted.

A shudder ran through her.

The last thing they wanted was another Leland.

Before Leland had broken ranks, things had followed a set routine: nineteen Guardians to watch over the Marrow, to send reluctant quiddity to its shores, to make sure that everyone who went stayed there, regardless of the decision they made.

It was a one-way street, always had been—it *had* to be a one-way street.

The alternative was nearly unthinkable.

Nineteen Guardians.

But then, one by one, Leland had started hunting down the others, murdering them in their sleep, in their homes, with their families, wherever he tracked them to.

Vicious, brutal crimes that only a madman could justify.

There were only a handful of them left, but if Leland had any say in the matter—and so far he most definitely did—then it was only a matter of time before their cards were punched, too.

Including hers.

And most likely the orphans sitting before her, who had, against all odds, somehow managed to escape his grasp the first time around.

"Okay, children," she said to the class, for her benefit as much as theirs. It did her no good to dwell on the past; the children before her were the future.

She tapped the sanded tree branch against the dark green chalkboard, causing a puff of chalk powder to add to the dust that already filled the air. With a flick of her wrist, she underlined the cursive text, ignoring the screeching sound that its imperfect tip made on the hard surface. "Who can read what this says?"

She scanned the children's faces, her eyes moving from the oldest, a boy named Kent, to two of the youngest: her own two boys.

When no one jumped at the opportunity to answer, she sighed and rubbed her eyes with the hand not holding the pointer, trying to clear some of the dirt and dust that threatened to obscure her vision. Then she took a deep breath.

It's not their fault, they're trying hard—they're working *hard. And they've already been through hell.*

And despite their efforts, things were progressing far too slowly for her liking. The longer that they spent together, the more likely it was that Leland would eventually find them.

She wouldn't let that happen—*couldn't* let that happen.

"It's the Book," she said softly, urging them on with her eyes.

A boy with straight black hair held his hand up high.

"*Inter mortuos et vivos,*" he replied with a lisp. He was one of the youngest of the orphans, barely five years of age. They had found him at the side of the road while his house burned to the foundation, his parents' screams still audible over the snapping and popping of the burning wood.

Sean had gotten to him before he was dropped into the system.

"No, not quite. Anyone else?"

A small smile crossed her face when the boy with the short brown hair put his hand up next.

"Yes?"

The boy didn't look up.

"*Inter vivos et mortuos,*" he said in his high-pitched four-year-old voice. "It means, *Between Life and Death.*"

The woman's smirk became a full-blown smile. A physical manifestation of pride, if there ever was one.

"That's right, that's right. And what is the title referring to?"

"The Marrow," the boy whispered, "where every person must make a choice."

"And what's in the book?"

"A prophecy." His voice was even smaller now, barely audible. "About a rift, an opening, and demons flooding backward—arriving here on Earth."

The woman's smile faded and she swallowed hard. The boy was right, of course, but that did nothing the dampen the images that flooded her mind.

"Correct. Now, Robert, would you please—?"

The woman stopped abruptly, tilting her face skyward. She had felt something in her chest, a minor tremor, like an arrhythmia.

She had felt this before.

Her eyes went wide and she turned her gaze to the door. A split second later, the worn, warped wood was thrown wide and Sean, red-faced, sweat beading on his brow, burst through.

"He's here!" he shouted, sprinting toward her. "He found us!"

The woman's entire body suddenly felt as if it were encased in ice.

Leland is here—my husband has found us.

Shoving the fear aside, the woman turned to the children, their expressions matching her own: pure horror. She doubted that they knew who the *he* Sean was referring to was, but they were reacting to *her*.

And she was reacting to the nearly crushing sensation in her chest.

He's here.

The woman tried to calm her now racing heart, to keep her emotions in check, to direct the orphans to behave in an orderly fashion, as if subjected to a fire drill.

He's here.

She failed.

"Get up!" the woman shouted. "Get the fuck up and *run!*"

Part I - The Dead Have Thoughts, Too

Chapter 1

EDWARD GRAY, KNOWN TO nearly everyone as Ed the Nose, had seen many a heinous crime in his twelve years as a New York City detective.

He had, after all, worked a case in which a man had murdered sixteen people over the course of a decade and chopped their bodies up into itty-bitty pieces and left them around Central Park as pigeon food.

They probably would never have caught him, if it hadn't been for an overzealous seagull pooping an entire index finger into the center of a flash mob.

But somehow, this case was worse—*the* worst, maybe.

Some said that working as a homicide detective hardened you, conditioned you to the worst types of crimes, of human depravity, that it turned a living breathing human into an organic shell of a being.

But not Edward. If anything, his job had made him a more compassionate individual, one that cared much for his fellow man, victims and even perpetrators. When he shared this view, the most common response, including from his once partner Pauley Ruddick, was always in the form of a question: *'Why do you care so much? Why try so damn hard to be* good, *when there is just so much* bad *all around us?'*

Ed had expended considerable thought on his answer over the years, and yet the only thing he could come up with was childish in nature, one small step above *'because.'*

Ed just flipped the script, posing the exact same question to Pauley, only he switched the word *do* to *don't*.

'Why don't *you care so much?'*

This response had predictably driven Pauley nearly insane, which, of course, had never been his intention. The truth was, deep down, Ed knew that everyone was essentially good. Evolution made them so; altruism, giving, caring, loving—these were characteristics built into the human soul, a necessary by-product of evolution that facilitated their success as a species.

As for the despicable murderers, rapists, and terrorists that he had dealt with over the years?

Ed considered them good, too. Only these people had a disease, one for which the prison system definitely wasn't a cure.

The simple fact was that there *was* no cure for what ailed these people, at least not yet. They were sick, plain and simple. And yet he still had a job to do, an obligation to keep the greater population safe from these infected.

Ed stared down at the photograph of the woman lying in the cage. It was a close-up of her face, and it was perhaps the most disturbing of the images. The three other people who had seen the photos—the photographer, the PD that discovered them, and of course, his boss, Gerry Trudemont—had all said that the woman's hands, which were bitten—*eaten*—to the bone were the worst.

Ed disagreed.

In the close-up of the woman's face, her eyes were open just enough for him to make out the lower crescents of her gray irises, her cheeks were gaunt and sallow, and her mouth, once pretty, was open as if by affect.

Her eyes—that was what got to Ed most. He knew that this woman's eyes had seen her impending death, her doom, and there was nothing that she could do about it but acquiesce, accept that horrible reality. Ed wasn't sure what the worst way to die was, and despite having heard over the years that that dubious title had been championed by drowning, he wasn't so sure. It was a fool's errand, trying to figure that one out, as no one had ever returned with a detailed report outlining what it felt like to actually die. Regardless, he was fairly certain that starving to death, having your body eat itself from the inside out, wasn't a good way to go.

With a sigh, he reached for the Styrofoam cup of stale coffee and took a swig. It was cold, and he swallowed the sludge with a grimace.

Logic decreed that the man who had done this to the woman in the photograph was a psychopath, someone who had a history of such acts. And by extension, logic also decreed that such a person didn't just up and leave when they had what he probably considered a perfect meal waiting for them at home.

And then there was the expense paid to create the false floor, the cage, the intricate setup.

And that said nothing of the tapes they had found.

The ones of the other victims, of Michael Grant Young eating them alive.

Edward shuddered, his eyes flicking to the enlarged image of Michael from his work ID card.

He's sick—a sick, sick man. But he is not a bad person.

This time, however, his inner voice took some convincing. Michael looked like a staple of American Wall Street: tall, dark, handsome, perfectly groomed. Expensive clothes, expensive cars, expensive condo, psychopathic tastes. A real, twenty-first-century American Psycho.

"Where did you go?" Ed muttered. "*Why* did you go?"

When dealing with psychopaths like Michael, the two most likely answers were either that he was incarcerated for another offense, or that he met someone meaner and badder than himself.

But as far as Ed could tell, neither of these were the case for Michael.

"Ed, heading out to get some lunch—a nice street sausage. You want?"

Ed looked up from the photos and rubbed his eyes.

Detective Hugh Freeman was the youngest in their district, having just made detective three months ago. He was too green to put on any cases yet; instead, he was working as a tag-along for the foreseeable future. He was not unlike Michael, Ed realized, save of course the shaggy blond hair. Hugh was in his mid-thirties, good-looking, in shape and healthy, the street meat notwithstanding.

Ed thought of his own body, about the fact that in his forty plus years he had drank a little too much and now had at least twenty pounds to lose, all of which was concentrated around his middle. And while Michael and Hugh's suits were probably bespoke, Ed wore the same wool blend sportscoat he had worn for years.

Hugh waved a hand over Ed's desk.

"Ed? You all right? Kinda zoned out back there."

Ed just stared.

"Well, I'm getting a sausage." He hooked a thumb over his shoulder to indicate that he was going to leave. "You want one? Something? Anything to fill that tire of yours?"

Ed smirked, but shook his head.

Sarcastic bastard. You wait until you've been in the game for as long as I have…we'll see then who looks like an extra on Baywatch.

"I'm good," he replied. His eyes darted to the photograph of the woman's face, to her cold, gray eyes. "Not hungry. When you get back, come see me, okay? I want to show you something."

The man's face lit up. He was eager as they came, which was another difference between them; the job had also taught Ed to be a master of patience.

But he couldn't fault the man for being enthusiastic. Shit, he had been that way once.

As Hugh left, Ed turned his attention back to the photograph of Michael Young.

You may be sick, but you still need to pay for what you have done. And I will find you, Michael, no matter where you are.

Chapter 2

"YOU'RE *WHAT?*" ROBERT NEARLY shouted. He couldn't believe his ears. It didn't make sense...and it was the last thing that he would have thought to come out of Shelly's mouth at that moment. A split second before confronting her about the photograph that he had found of her in Father Callahan's church, she'd dropped *this* bombshell.

She said she's pregnant, Helen said inside his head.

"Thanks," he replied with a grimace.

Shelly looked at him like he was having a schizoid break reminiscent of Andrew Shaw.

"I said I was pregnant, Robert. I—I don't know how it happened."

Cal stepped forward, his round face an inhuman shade of white. He looked like he had seen a ghost...or many of them.

"Guys, we gotta talk about this later. First, we've gotta get rid of this body, before the shit comes back. And then we need to find out how the hell we are going to get Allan back."

At the mention of the kid's name, Robert glanced to the spot near the center of the room where he had been standing before the quiddity had wrapped her arms around him.

How the fuck...?

Then he remembered Helen, and the fact that it had been she who had sent Allan on his way, and Robert stopped the thought before it came to fruition.

It hadn't been her; she had been under Carson or Leland's control.

Despite his best efforts, he realized that he was going to have to do a better job of keeping his thoughts to himself; his mind flashed orange.

You promised, Helen reminded him. *You promised you would send me back.*

Robert shook his head, trying to regain some semblance of control, to strengthen his tenuous grip on sanity.

"Fuck...pregnant? You sure?"

Shelly looked at him, her expression souring.

"I'm sure. And this is not exactly the reaction I was hoping for."

Robert bit his tongue. He had so much that he had to say, and even more he had to ask, but now was not the time.

Cal was right, they had to do something with the steaming corpse in the Mickey Mouse t-shirt lying behind them.

Shelly, as if she were in his head instead of Helen, addressed the issue with her signature bluntness. "Burn him."

This time, however, Robert didn't feel the need to chide her for her callousness. She was right. He remembered something that Sean had said during one of his previous visits, about burying the body deep enough or cremating them. Either would work.

Sean.

Just the thought of the man's name nearly made his blood boil.

He shook the thought from his head, and turned his attention to the task at hand.

Burning him would mean, of course, that Leland would get another of his horrible henchmen back on his side of the Marrow, but there was nothing they could do about that. Besides, it was better with him *there* than *here*.

He also has Amy and Allan.

"Fuck," he grumbled, gritting his teeth against the frustration that threatened to once again put him into a rage. It was all an endless cycle: the bad guys came to kill them, or worse, to use Robert to open the rift, and if the good guys won, the bad guys just got a first-class ticket back to their malicious leader.

The least Robert could do was send them as burnt offerings.

"Burn him," he said with a nod, pushing thoughts of Sean, of Shelly and her pregnancy, aside for the time being. "Cal, you want to grab one leg, and I'll grab the other?"

Cal nodded, and together they strode over to the man's fallen body. Robert tried not to look directly at the hole in the center of his body, the gaping orifice that obliterated Mickey Mouse's face.

Just as he bent down to grab one of the man's chubby ankles, he instantly shot back up again.

With everything that had happened tonight, and him being so blinded by trying to save Shelly and Allan, and to fight off Carson, he hadn't even stopped to consider where the shot had come from—or, perhaps more importantly, who had taken it.

His eyes darted to the shattered window at the back of the room, and he peered out into the night.

He saw only a thin crescent of a moon casting foggy rays down on the Harlop Estate.

Steeling himself for the gore, Robert turned back to the massive hole in the fat man's body.

This was no regular pistol round; shit, it wasn't even from a machine gun like the ones that the men had used at Seaforth. No, this was a high-powered rifle of some sort, clearly military grade.

And there was only one person that Robert could think of who might have access to such a gun, or even know how to use it.

"You collect a friend on your travels, Robert?" Cal asked, clearly thinking the same thing.

Robert shook his head.

"No, not a friend. But I'm pretty sure I know who took the shot. The only thing I don't understand is *why*—and why he didn't take another," he replied, thinking of when the other man had jumped on top of him and bitten off part of his finger.

Remembering the snap the sound the man's teeth had made when it broke his skin made his stomach lurch, and he avoided looking directly at any of his own injuries.

Deep down, he knew his ear, stomach, ankle, chest, and finger were going to bring him agony in the coming days, but with everything that had happened, culminating with Shelly's pregnancy, it almost seemed an afterthought.

He was numb.

"Who was it?" Shelly demanded, making her way over to them. She was still shirtless, and he couldn't help but stare at her bare belly. It wasn't a bump, per se, just some extra skin around her middle.

Thinking back, he remembered the last time they had had sex, the time when Allan had first come to the Estate, and realized that she must have been going on about four months now.

He swallowed hard. Everything was happening so fast.

"Robert? Who killed this fucking scumbag?" Shelly asked as she walked right on top of the man on the ground. Unlike he and Cal, she didn't seem all that disturbed by the links of entrails spilling out of the man's body.

Probably because she was happy that he was gone.

If I'd come in a few minutes later…

Robert forced the thought from his head.

"I'll tell you later—but for now, why don't you go on and take a shower? Get cleaned up. Cal and I will deal with the body."

Shelly pursed her lips, and he feared that she was going to be obstinate again, that she would refuse out of principle, if nothing else. But when she spoke next, he realized that he had misjudged her reaction.

"Is it safe?" she asked in a small voice.

Robert turned his thoughts inward. He no longer felt any pressure in his chest, in his core, and there was no sensation of time slowing.

And then as further confirmation, Helen's thoughts mimicked his own.

"It's safe," he replied. He cleared his throat and repeated the phrase. "It's safe, Shel."

Shelly nodded, and it was as if that simple sentence sapped her of her energy. She looked exhausted.

Without another word, she spun and left the room, leaving Robert to watch her go.

Pregnant.

Robert shook his head, and reached down and grabbed the man's fat ankle in both hands. Then he turned to Cal.

"Ready? Let's go burn this fucker—send him back to hell."

Chapter 3

"YOU EVER BEEN ON a case like this? I mean, as a grunt—have you ever seen anything this bad?" Ed asked, his eyes trained on the road.

"Nothing this bad, no," Hugh admitted. Out of the corner of his eye, Ed saw the man shrug. "We had this one case, went cold after fifteen years before it was solved. Pretty fucked up shit, missing kids 'n all that. But nothing like *this.*"

Ed remained silent; his question had served its purpose. It had been designed to see if Hugh was aware of how fucked up this whole situation actually was: a man keeping women in his dungeon of a basement, in a cage, eating them while they were still alive.

It was incredibly *fucked* up.

Hugh's ho-hum attitude suggested that either he was in shock or this kind of shit didn't bother the younger generation the way it affected even someone as experienced as Ed. Either way, in the very least it meant that the man would be able to function.

Whether or not he would be of use, however, had yet to be determined.

Thinking about the details of the horrible crimes committed by Michael Young, Ed pushed the pedal a little harder. His longstanding relationship with the media had been stressed to the limit with this case; he had to go see some the higherups to make sure that the details remained quiet. Leaking little tidbits of information like breadcrumbs wasn't the news outlets' favorite thing to do, and Ed knew that it was only a matter of time before the entire story emerged.

Over the past few years, Ed had seen the news go from the subtle nuances of a John LeCarre novel to a Michael Bay film — car crashes and explosions and all the substance of an emaciated chicken wing.

And now there was more than just the media to contend with. All it took was a scumbag with a cell phone and a long-range mic, and the jig was up. When the public found out about the horrors on Wall Street, the fact that an animal like Michael Young lived among them, under their noses, well…he could see the headline now: Horror on Wall Street.

Meh, creativity wasn't his strong suit.

That was the thing; the general public wanted to believe that crimes such as this one happened like in the movies: a mutant hillbilly buried deep in the woods that murdered and tortured only those who came a-calling.

As if someone being curious made them deserving of their fate; or, in the very least, that was what they told themselves.

But Ed knew better.

In all of his years, he hadn't seen it. The myth of the hermit murderer was simply that: a myth.

Most often, the perp was a sociopath living an otherwise normal life, one who by virtue of their disease inflicted mayhem on people they didn't even know.

And this was terrifying to most people, almost unthinkable.

"Where we going, anyway?" Hugh asked, breaking the uncomfortable silence inside the car.

Ed sighed.

"We're going to Michael's office."

"His office? Why? Local PD has already spoken to all of his colleagues—nothing doing. He worked alone, as the profile suggests."

Ed was well aware of the facts in this case, so he elected not to respond. Hugh followed his lead, and the rest of the drive toward Michael's office was quiet, which was fine by Ed. Hugh, on the other hand, seemed uncomfortable; the man played with his phone, shifted in his seat, did pretty much everything he could do short of breaking the silence.

The downtown core was a predictable log jam, but when Ed took a side road that clearly didn't lead to the man's office, Hugh could hold his tongue no longer.

"His office is up on 31st," he said matter-of-factly.

Ed elected to remain silent. He pulled his Taurus up to a small park, driving half onto the curb to prevent blocking traffic on the narrow street, and stopped the car. Then he opened his door, but before stepping out, Hugh called after him.

"Look, I don't mean to be rude, Ed. I respect you, and your nose—maybe not so much your wardrobe—but I can't see how this is helping me learn the ropes. I mean, if you won't even speak to me...what am I supposed to do?"

His back to Hugh, Ed allowed himself a small smirk.

"You listen, Hugh. You just watch and you listen."

***

The park was quiet, which was a good thing—it meant that if Michael had wanted to speak to someone out of sight, but didn't want to stray so far from the office that he couldn't head back after lunch, then this would be the place.

But what was obvious to Ed seemed above Hugh's paygrade.

"What are we doing here, Ed?"

Ed shook his head, wishing that the man would just shut up and sit there in silence. For the better part of an hour they had been sitting on different benches, as per his instruction, with two empty ones between them. During that time, several people had passed through the park, yet despite straddling noon, no one had actually come and sit down. Ed himself was getting hungry, and although he had oodles more patience than his partner, he didn't know if he could hold out for more than another hour or so without getting something into his considerable belly.

But when the woman in her eighties, dressed in a Gucci jacket, her ears and throat adorned with pearls, came into the park, he knew he wouldn't have to wait much longer.

He looked over at Hugh, who stared back, an eyebrow raised. Ed held his hand out, indicating for him to stay put. As of yet, the woman hadn't noticed either of them, which was another good sign. It meant that the park was typically quiet, that the woman wearing the oversized sunglasses didn't expect to see anyone.

Which also meant that if someone *had* been here—a sharp-dressed power broker, for instance—then she might have taken notice.

The woman walked her small dog over to a patch of grass not ten feet from where Ed sat on the bench.

"Go on, Tootsie, do your business. Mama doesn't have all day."

The dog, a pint-sized ball of brown fur, did a little circle, then squatted on its tiny, quivering haunches and dropped a dime-sized piece of shit on the grass.

"That's a good girl," the woman said, and then quickly followed up with some unintelligible cooing noises.

Tootsie suddenly looked up, and when her beady black eyes met Ed's, the thing yapped.

"Wha—?"

Then the woman caught sight of Ed and Hugh, and if her face hadn't undergone dozens of rounds of plastic surgery over the years, the former would have expected her features to drop. Instead, she stood upright and pushed her sunglasses higher up her needle-thin nose.

"C'mon, Tootsie, let's go," she said quickly, giving the dog's leash a tug. The dog remained rooted. "Tootsie, I said let's go!"

When Tootsie still didn't listen, she hurried over and scooped her up with thin arms.

"Ma'am! Ma'am!" Ed said, finally rising. He gestured for Hugh to follow.

"I'm sorry, I don't have any change!" the woman shouted back, turning quickly on her heels.

Ed stifled a chuckle. Maybe his sportscoat *was* that bad.

"Ma'am, please, I just have a few questions."

The woman didn't look back; instead, she shuffled her Louboutins across the sidewalk and out of the park.

"Leave me alone! I'll call the police…I swear, I'll scream."

Ed hurried after her. Even though she must have been pushing eighty, he was breathing heavily by the time he caught up to her.

She must have heard him approach, because when he came within a foot, she whipped around.

Ed half expected her to be holding a can of Mace in her thin fingers. Thankfully, it was only a cellphone.

"Police! I'll call—"

Ed flashed his detective shield.

"No need, ma'am; we're already here."

Chapter 4

THE SMELL WAS HORRENDOUS, and yet Robert couldn't bring himself to move away from the body.

He wanted to make sure that it all burnt.

Robert knew that the bones wouldn't be reduced to ash, wouldn't burn in the makeshift fire that they had built in the backyard, but they had plans for those afterward.

But the rest of it would.

It was times like these that he was glad that the Harlop Estate was as isolated as it was. By the time the thick, dark clouds from Jonah Silvers's rendering fat reached any of the neighbors, it would have dissipated into the atmosphere.

At most, someone might think that he was having a midnight barbecue; strange, but not 'call the police' strange.

And yet, this offered him little comfort. He would have been lying if he'd said that, standing over the body as the man's chest hair crackled and burnt away and his eyes sizzled before popping, his level of comfort around what was undeniably grotesque wasn't disturbing.

Oh, how far he had come—or gotten lost—since being an accountant for Audex Accounting.

"Who was it, Rob?" Cal asked quietly. Like Robert, his eyes were trained on the burning body, but by firelight, Robert knew that the man was still very much affected by what had happened inside the Harlop Estate.

It was odd, what with Robert having a greater constitution than his best friend.

Robert chewed his lip for a moment before answering. He had left both Cal and Shelly because he didn't want them to get any more involved in this mess than they already were. But in the end, it was his return that had saved them.

His return with a piece of his ear missing, a gash down the center of his chest, a twisted ankle, and now a missing finger, but his return nonetheless.

And now that Shelly was pregnant, he couldn't imagine leaving them again anytime soon.

They were in this together, it seemed.

For better or for worse, they were a trio.

Trio…

His thoughts turned to Allan and the look of sheer horror on his face as he faded.

Should be a quad — we should be a fucking *quad.*

An orange light flashed in his mind.

Quint, Helen reminded him, *but hopefully not for long.*

Robert nodded.

When the silence went on for too long, Cal turned to him.

"What happened out there, Robert? Where did you go?"

He should have known that Cal's outburst before Seaforth was as far as the man would go. Cal was fiercely loyal, and while he harbored a dark secret of his own, Robert knew that he would always be by his side.

Still, loyal as he was, there was pain in his friend's voice — pain and betrayal.

Robert sighed.

"I found the book, Cal. I had the —" He held his palms out in front of him, then stared skyward. Through the thick black smoke, he saw a sprinkling of stars in the night sky above. For a brief second, they reminded him of the flecks of the Marrow Sea that appeared when he closed his eyes, salting the pepper darkness.

"I had the *Inter vivos et mortuos* in my hands, Cal. In my—"
His voice hitched, and he fought back tears. "—in my hands I
held the book. And then it was taken away from me. That *bastard* Sean and his men..." He let his sentence trail off.

*The same bastard man that saved me and Shelly from Jonah Sil-
vers.*

For a moment, Cal said nothing. Then he took a deep breath
and replied in a hushed tone.

"What about it, Robbo? What do you think that this book is
going to do for you? Why is it so important?"

The response caught Robert off guard.

"What will it do for *me*? No, no, not for *me*—for *her*, Cal. In
it, there is a way to get her back. I know it."

"You *know* it? How do you know it? Look, I get that you're
special 'n all that, Robbo, but how do you know? It's just a fucking book."

"It's not *just* a book, Cal. It was a way to get Amy back."

Cal shrugged; he didn't need to say anything else, because
Robert hadn't answered his question the first or even the second time.

The truth was, Robert couldn't answer because there were
some secrets he still refused to share.

*How do I know? I know because Father Callahan told me to get the
book. He told me right before I shot him in the head.*

That's how I know.

The irony of the fact that Cal, he of conspiracy theories ranging from 9/11 being an inside job to chemtrails, was trying to
talk some sense into him was not beyond Robert.

But that didn't make him right, either.

There was a fizzle from the fire, and the flames suddenly
died down. Jonah's clothes and skin were gone, and the wet-
ness of his organs beneath had calmed the fire. Cal walked a

couple steps behind them and retrieved a gas can. Then he returned and leaned over the smoldering body. After what looked like a moment of contemplation, he poured the entire gas can on the flames.

The blaze burned so hot and bright that Robert was forced to shield his eyes. The fiery spire only lasted a few seconds before all of the gas was gone again, leaving in its wake a glowing hot outline of what had once been Jonah Silvers.

"I don't want to sound insensitive, Robbo, really I don't—I can't imagine what you've been through. I mean, shit, while I've been through hell, you've been there and back—twice."

Robert didn't think that his friend's observation deserved an answer, so he remained silent. Besides, he had a feeling that something more was coming, something that would incite a response.

"But...but you gotta let go, man," Cal was speaking quickly now, giving Robert no chance to interject. "Let go of Amy—it's been, what? A year? Two? And now that Shelly's pregnant, and your fucking brother and some of his homo psychos are out to get us, don't you think it's about time to let go?"

Robert swallowed hard, trying to keep his emotions in check as he mulled over his friend's words. The preamble to this whole diatribe long forgotten, he struggled not to lose control.

Calm, be calm.

This time he didn't know if the thought was his or Helen's.

He closed his eyes, but the fire still burned bright behind his lids.

"She's my daughter, Cal—and she's there, with *him*," was his only reply. In a strange way, he was proud of himself for not flying off the handle.

Cal nodded, and he kicked a smoldering piece of something or other back toward the main fire.

"Then I guess we need to get that book back," the man said simply.

This response, much like his own, surprised Robert, and he looked over at his friend, whose cheeks were glistening with tears. He wanted so much to go to the man, to hold him tight in his arms, but something kept him at bay.

"Cal, I wanted to th—"

But a voice from behind him caused him to freeze.

"I can help you find the book, Robert. I can help."

Chapter 5

"JUST GIVE ME THE ticket, then, because I'm not picking up the scat."

Ed laughed. He couldn't help it. The woman truly was clueless.

Really? A detective giving her a ticket for not picking up her dog's shit?

"Listen lady, I don't care about the dog shit, okay?" The curse word had the desired effect; the woman's lips pressed together tightly.

"Then what is that you want?"

"I just—"

The woman held up the hand not wrapped around the dog that was nuzzled into her arm like a running back cradling a football.

"No, you know what? I'm not answering any questions without my lawyer present." As if to reinforce the point, the lady shook her head defiantly.

Ed rolled his eyes, which, in retrospect, was the absolutely wrong thing to do. The woman's eyes darted down at Ed's hand, which was still lightly holding her forearm.

He yanked it back as if it were scalded. Something brushed up against his shoulder, and he snapped his head around.

It was Hugh, and he was smiling, of all things.

"What's—" *wrong with you,* he intended to say, but the man cut him off.

"Ed, please, let me speak to the nice lady." His smile grew, revealing perfectly white teeth. "Please."

Ed squinted, shrugged, and then stepped aside.

There was no way that this woman was going to talk to him anyway, so why not let Hugh take the brunt of her disgust for the lower-middle class?

And how dare a vermin such as Detective Edward Gray touch her Gucci coat?

"Firstly, ma'am—or missus, do you prefer missus?"

Ed raised an eyebrow at his partner.

Missus?

"Ma'am is fine."

"Yes, okay, ma'am. So, first of all, I want to apologize for our behavior earlier. We've just been a little jumpy lately, is all."

The woman's pursed face remained, but some of the creases around her mouth seemed to transition from crevices to ravines.

'Bout time for another collagen injection, ma'am.

"What is this about, Mr....?"

Hugh's smile grew, and he brushed a lock of blond hair off his forehead.

"Hugh, Detective Hugh Freeman. And this is about just a question or two—"

Her eyes clouded again.

What the hell is with this woman?

Hugh held up his hands defensively.

"No, no need to be alarmed. All me and my partner want to know is if you saw someone here a couple of weeks ago. That's it. It has nothing at all to do with you, and you are in no way in trouble. In fact, you can walk away right now, if you want, and you won't ever see us again. I promise."

The woman looked suspicious, but to Ed's utmost surprise, she didn't take Hugh up on the offer to leave.

"Here? If I saw someone in this park?"

"Yep. This park. It would have been about two weeks ago. Now I know how memory can—"

"My memory is sharp, young man. And I come here, through this park, every single day around this time."

Now Ed smirked. He was impressed by the young man's approach; it was calm, collected, calculated. Hugh was impatient as hell, but at least he had this going for him. Ed tried to remember if he had ever been this smooth.

Doubtful.

But then again, he had never looked like a surfer in a bespoke suit, either—so it wasn't exactly his fault.

"Well then maybe you can remember two Tuesdays ago—" He glanced at Ed. "My partner and I aren't sure, but there might have been a man here, a man in a suit—Wall Street types, you know the kind."

The woman frowned and adjusted her grip on the dog in the crook of her elbow.

"The *'type'*? My grandson is one of the top traders in—"

"Good-looking?"

"Yes."

Hugh slipped a finger down the lapel of his suit jacket.

"Dresses well?"

"Yes."

"Good manners?"

"Of course."

Hugh smiled again.

"That's the type I meant. You must be very proud of your grandson."

"I am."

"So...did you see anyone by that description here? Two weeks ago?"

The women seemed to ponder this.

"No, I didn't see anyone like my grandson."

Hugh shrugged.

"So that's that, then. Thank you very much for your—"

The woman held up a finger.

"Wait, wait. There was a man in a suit, but his tie was all messy, and his hair? That was a mess, too. My grandson would never allow himself to be seen like that this close to the offices."

Ed's ears perked up. Things had suddenly gotten significantly more interesting.

"Had you ever seen this man before? I mean, on all your—" Ed started, but Hugh held up his hand, silencing him.

"Ma'am, can you tell me how or why you might remember something like that?"

"Well, first of all, there is usually no one here at this park at lunch, or barely ever, anyway. But it was the other two that were with him—" She shuddered before continuing, "I normally come right here, let Tootsie do her business, then head back to my penthouse. But this time, I got one look at them and turned right around. Got out of here as fast as I could. This is New York, you know; you can't be too careful."

Ed grunted.

You don't know the half of it.

"Wait, there were two other men with him? Can you...can you remember something about them? Anything?"

"Oh, yeah, I can. Like I said, my memory is just fine, and those two...those two left an *impression*."

She paused, her head tilting slightly upward and to the left.

"The first, he was this fat, balding thing, wearing a Disney shirt of some kind, and he had these tiny, beady eyes, you know? That was a bad man, I could tell that from the second I saw him. And I'm not talking snatch an old lady's purse bad."

She made a face, and this time she definitely shuddered. "But the other one...the other one was worse."

"Please," Hugh said, reaching out and touching her arm gently. "Anything you can tell us will be very helpful."

"Yes...the other man was thin, gaunt, looked like he hadn't slept in days. Deep, dark circles around his eyes, you know?"

Hugh nodded, encouraging her to continue.

"And he was...I, I don't know—he was smiling a lot, but only with his mouth. His eyes definitely weren't smiling. No, I don't think that man has really smiled in a long, long time."

Hugh looked over at Ed and gave him a wink. A *wink*, of all things.

Cocky bastard.

But inside, Ed was smiling too. They were getting somewhere.

Chapter 6

WHEN ROBERT RECOGNIZED THE voice, he immediately threw his hands in the air.

"Don't shoot!"

Cal, his face a mask of confusion, whipped around.

"Don't shoot? Don't shoot? Who the fuck—?"

But he must have seen something that took his breath away.

"You!" he said, his voice dropping from a shout to a whisper.

"I'm not...I'm not here to hurt you," Aiden replied.

Something brushed against his arm, and Robert jumped.

"Robbo, turn the fuck around."

Robert, realizing that it was just Cal who had grabbed him, did as his friend instructed.

It was difficult to make out much, what with their bodies blocking the glow from the fire behind them, but the man that stood before them was most definitely Aiden, complete with a wad of chaw tucked in his lower lip. But there was something different about him, something that he couldn't quite place.

But Robert didn't have time to give this much thought; he was more concerned with what appeared to be a sniper rifle slung over the man's shoulder.

"You shot Jonah," Robert said softly. Images of the hideous troll on top of Shelly came flooding back to him, and he felt a pang deep down in his stomach. "Thank you; thank you for that."

The man said nothing; he simply spat a stream of tobacco juice onto the ground between them.

"No, really. I can't—"

"The man told me to keep an eye on you, so I did."

Cal appeared less grateful than Robert.

"Yeah, and what about the other fucker? The freak who ate part of Robert's finger? How about him, huh? What happened there? And Carson? The bitch with the knife? What about them? Did 'the man' tell you to stop giving a shit after taking out the fat one?"

"Easy, Cal," Robert said, his eyes still locked on Aiden. There was something about the way that the little light that reached him seemed strange, like a trompe-l'oeil.

He glanced over to Cal and noticed that the light bounced off him with a sort of iridescent quality. But with Aiden, it seemed to dull.

"No, don't 'easy' me. This guy was supposed to protect us, and he fucking failed."

Cal's words didn't phase Aiden; in fact, he didn't seem to even acknowledge the man's anger.

"He didn't fail us," Robert said softly. He felt a stirring in his mind, and a flash of orange.

Helen was back, but Robert pushed her down again.

I know.

Cal turned to him now, and Robert was reminded of the way he had stormed off before Seaforth. Cal was a much angrier man than he'd ever remembered. His best friend had always been a little off, eager to latch on to conspiracy theories, but he was never *angry*, at least not like this.

"Calm down, Cal, please."

"Nope, not gonna do it. This fucker *failed* us. You hear that, big shot? All your—"

Robert reached out and squeezed his friend's arm, hard. Cal's anger was clearly misplaced; it wasn't as if they had hired this man, or had even known that he was outside the Harlop Estate when everything had gone down.

"What the fuck, Robbo?"

"Cal, be quiet."

The man's face went dark.

"Don't—"

Robert didn't give him a chance.

"He didn't fail us, you idiot. He failed himself, protecting us."

Cal recoiled.

"What? What the hell are you—?"

"He's dead," Robert said flatly. "Aiden's dead."

***

"They snuck up on me. I let my guard down for one minute, maybe less, and they snuck up on me. I knew that he was there, of course, but I didn't plan for the girl. And my god, she was fast."

Aiden seemed almost apathetic, although Robert wasn't certain how one was supposed to feel or sound or even look when talking about their own death. In fact, aside from Helen in his head and maybe Dr. Mansfield, Aiden was the only normal dead person that he had ever spoken to.

"I'm sorry, Aiden. And—" Robert gestured to Cal and Shelly, who were sitting on the couch opposite the gray man. "—and we want to thank you for helping us."

Shelly, who looked nearly as monochrome as the quiddity across from them despite having showered and gotten dressed, swallowed hard. Robert could tell that she wanted to reach out and grab Aiden, to thank the man for getting Jonah off her, but that, of course, was out of the question.

Robert nodded to her, then turned back to Aiden.

"Why...why...why do you know what happened to you? I mean, you were there at Seaforth with all the others—they had no idea that they were dead."

Aiden opened his mouth to answer, but to Robert's surprise it wasn't his words that he heard, but Helen's in his mind, telling her own story.

It was a confusing mess. I knew that there was something wrong, that something wasn't quite right, but I couldn't place it. Like a word that you mean to say, that you want to say, but just can't get it out. And then, when that thing—the Goat—spoke to me, I had no choice but to listen. I don't know how—

Robert tried to soothe her with calm thoughts.

Helen was right, of course; it *was* confusing.

Confusing and overwhelming.

He glanced over at Shelly, and seeing his own bewilderment mirrored on her pretty, round face, Robert knew that he had to be the one to be strong. Not Cal, not Shelly, not even Allan, wherever he was.

But him.

Robert Thomas *Black*.

"I don't know," Aiden said with a shrug. "I don't know."

"And why...how did you come back so fast? With the others..."

Aiden shrugged again and continued to stare straight ahead.

Robert took a moment, trying not to upset the man. Yet, looking at him and his flat expression, he wasn't sure that Aiden was capable of such an emotion.

Most men, Robert presumed, would have been angry after what had happened to Aiden, furious even. But not him.

Cal interlaced his fingers, tapped his foot, and leaned forward on the couch. His tone had softened considerably since their encounter outside, and Robert thought that Cal had nearly returned to his old self.

"We can send you back," he whispered so softly that Robert barely picked up the words. "Robert can do it."

Aiden's eyes, previously clear if a little gray, suddenly flashed with darkness, like ink spilled into a glass of spring water.

"No, I don't want to go back—not just yet. I have something I have to do."

Maybe he is capable of anger after all, Helen thought. *But he's a good man, one that we should be glad to have on our side.*

Robert couldn't agree more.

He just needed to figure out how best to use him to find the book.

Chapter 7

"YOU BELIEVE IN GHOSTS, Hugh?"

"In what? Ghosts? Hell no."

"God?"

It was heavy talk for fifteen minutes postprandial, but Ed was so impressed with the way that Hugh had dealt with the woman in the park that he felt the need to get to know the man better.

And when Hugh had used the word 'partner,' as presumptuous as it had been, something had clicked inside Ed. He wasn't sure he was up for another one so soon given what had happened to his last one, but it was definitely something on the horizon. He could see a good yin and yang situation with the man, a complementary piece that might just fit.

A friend, maybe, although it had been so long since Ed had had one of those, he wasn't quite sure what it felt like anymore.

"No," Hugh replied. "No, I don't believe in God."

Ed continued to drive, moving farther away from the city and toward the suburbs. Twice Hugh had asked where the hell they were going, but his reply had been the same: watch and listen.

And answer questions, of course.

No matter how personal.

"Why not?"

Hugh shrugged and then unexpectedly opened up. Ed had thought the man's generation more guarded, what with 'safe places' and people getting offended at even the thought of a fart in public, but clearly Hugh was different.

And that was good, because Ed was different, too.

"I guess I can't believe in something that has never been proven, you know? I mean, we all believe in Santa Claus, the Easter Bunny, Tooth Fairy, and other fairy tales when we are young, but as time goes on we outgrow these myths. For whatever reason, however, this one myth, the myth of a Heaven and a Hell, of God and Satan, those persist. Rooted in our evolution, I suppose, but just a myth nonetheless."

Ed knew that over the past few years it had become a bit of a fad to call oneself an atheist or agnostic, but Hugh's response suggested a deeper layer of thought than just following a trend. Ed quickly glanced over at the man and tried to take him in, to understand his essence. Twelve years as an NYC detective, and nine more as a beat cop before that, had taught him much of the human condition. And with this knowledge came the ability to tease out the real, underlying individual beneath the skin they presented to the world.

And Hugh appeared to be more than just a pretty face and a fancy suit. There was something to him, some substance.

"You know, we look back at the Greek and Roman gods and immediately throw shade. 'Ah, those were stupid, how can someone believe a horse and carriage drag the sun up every morning?' My response is always that they had more conviction at the time; they believed so wholly that it was real that they would sacrifice children to these deities. *Sacrifice* them. And yet for some reason, only the religions of today are the ones that are quote-unquote *real*. Gimme a break. It's Santa Claus wearing long robes and preferring young boys to elves in green suits."

Ed smirked.

Tell me how you really feel, Hugh. Don't hold back now.

Hugh turned to face him, shock briefly crossing over his features as he realized for the first time that Ed was observing him.

He shrugged, as if to say, 'Meh, no big deal, not trying to offend.'

"What about you?"

Ed looked away, keeping his cards close to his chest. While he was adept at reading others, he liked to keep his own thoughts and feelings personal.

He hadn't always been this way, but his thoughts about everyone being good, that this was the default and that only errors and mutations made people do horrible things, had gotten a stiff upper lip from the older brass.

It was these comments that had probably cemented him as a career detective, never to rise in the ranks.

But now that he was the older brass, Ed tried hard not to pass judgment on Hugh.

He chuckled, trying to lighten the suddenly dark mood in the car.

"What about me?" he asked, his go-to refrain from times like these. It was annoying as all hell, a sentiment that was reflected in Hugh's expression, but it usually did the trick.

And this case was no exception.

They drove in silence for another half hour, the skyscrapers devolving into more modest offices, and then to apartment buildings. Ed had just pulled into a gas station when Hugh overcame his obvious annoyance and decided to speak up again, clearly choosing his words carefully. Thankfully, he changed the subject, reverting to a more professional approach.

"I get the fact that talking to the woman wasn't a waste of time…I mean, we know that there was a man who could possibly be Michael meeting a fat bald dude and a skinny guy with non-smiling eyes in the park during his lunch hour, from which he never returned. I'll tip my cap to you; potentially valuable information there. But you gotta help me out here…what are you thinking? If it was Michael, who were the other two? Was it gambling debts? Blackmail? Collaborators? How does this information get us any farther ahead, Ed?"

Ed thought about this for a moment; he definitely had a plan of attack, a reason if no rhyme to what he was doing. He just wasn't sure if he wanted to share it with Hugh.

Not just yet, anyway.

When Ed didn't answer, Hugh sighed and stared out the window. It wasn't the greatest start to their partnership, Ed supposed, but there was something to coming up with the plan yourself, of putting the pieces together on your own, that held incredible value.

Ed was reminded of a time long ago, back when his daughters were three and five. They loved puzzles, and he would often admire them as they worked together, trying to fit the pieces in place. For easy puzzles, the girls would pretty much share the work. But when things became difficult, his five-year-old daughter Haley would take over, and Jordynne would take a back seat. Haley would tell her where to put the pieces, order her even. It didn't matter if the piece would fit in or not; Jordynne would just jam it into place to make her sister happy.

He couldn't be certain, but Ed thought that this simple act had molded her to what she was to become, that it had shaped her personality.

Just the perfect mixture of gullibility and refraining from speaking up.

He swallowed hard, trying to push the image of his youngest daughter's face peeking out from behind those steel bars, her head shaved, her eyes sunken.

The god-awful orange jumpsuit.

He didn't want that to happen to Hugh; there was something to *doing* it for yourself, rather than being told or having your hand held while together you skip to the conclusion. And Ed couldn't help but think, no matter how childish, that he was getting a bit of a second chance here with Hugh.

And to think, this was all borne out of street meat, of Hugh asking him if he wanted a sausage while he pored over the photographs.

"Hey, wait," Hugh said, a tinge of excitement on his tongue, "isn't this the ATM where Michael took out three grand the last afternoon he was seen?"

Ed smiled and exited the vehicle.

Yeah, he was starting to learn, all right.

Hugh hurried after him.

"But, wait—we checked the ATM camera, nothing on it except for a stressed-looking Michael Young. Couldn't make out his car in the background, anything of interest—he didn't even go inside the station to take a piss."

Ed shook his head.

"No, *he* didn't," Ed said. He patted Hugh on the back. "Just watch and listen, Hugh. Watch and listen."

***

"It's all yours. The tapes from Tuesday are there on top," the man with the handlebar mustache said, indicating the stack of videotapes on the desk in the office at the back of the store. "Four cameras, two inside, two outside. One by the ATM."

"Tapes?" Hugh grumbled just loud enough for Ed to hear. "These guys still use tapes?"

Ed hushed him.

"Thank you, Mr....?"

"Edmonds."

"Huh, Ed and Edmonds."

"Pardon?"

Ed shook his head.

"Nothing."

That was another thing that Ed had strong thoughts about: coincidences. They didn't *just* happen. The Baader-Meinhof phenomenon and all that.

"Don't know what you think you're gonna find, though. Cops already went through it all. And I already gave a statement: didn't see no man in a suit. I'm lucky if my clientele is wearing a shirt."

Ed just smiled and thanked the man again. Then he gently guided Mr. Edmonds out of the room and shut the door.

Turning back to Hugh, he said, "You aren't going to let a neophyte like myself go through the tapes, are you? I'm more apt to erase them than find anything on them."

Hugh raised an eyebrow.

"Tapes? You think I have experience with VHS tapes? How old do you think I am?"

Ed laughed.

"Take a seat, start with the camera at the ATM, get a pic of our man."

Hugh turned back to the tapes, his hands outstretched. His frustration was palpable.

Deal with it.

If there was something else Ed had learned from this job was that frustration was nearly ubiquitous.

Hugh shifted the tapes around. From his vantage point near the door, Ed could only make out the date and a number written on them, which he assumed corresponded to the camera from which it was obtained.

"Which one? Christ—what's the point of this, Ed? The cops have already—"

"Just put a tape in and let's get started," Ed replied, leaning up against a dark brown cabinet. He noticed an unopened can of Coke on top and popped it. The carbonation tickled his tongue. "We're gonna be here a while, and the longer you take to get started, the more likely I am to develop some sort of glucose intolerance," he joked.

The truth was, Edward "Ed the Nose" Gray was already diabetic, had been for years.

Chapter 8

"FOUR OF US, THREE of them," Cal said. "Makes sense. *And* we have two cameras that are still working. Don't forget that."

Robert had bit his tongue for long enough. He shot to his feet.

"Cal, are you crazy? Shelly isn't going anywhere—she's staying here."

Now it was Shelly's turn to rise.

"I'm not letting you guys go alone."

Cal shook his head.

"Not this shit again. Robbo, she's a grown fucking woman, she can make her own decisions."

Wendy made her own choices, too, and look where that got her and Amy.

"I know you think you have to look after everyone, after...after..." Cal lowered his gaze and let his sentence trail off.

It didn't matter; he didn't have to say it. He knew what the man was thinking, but he wouldn't let him bring Amy back into this.

"She's pregnant, for Christ's sake! Think about someone other than yourself for once, Cal!"

Robert's blood was starting to boil. He was so fucking tired, he couldn't think straight. The only thing that seemed clear to him for some reason was Wendy's car accident, only it wasn't Wendy in the front seat, but Shelly. And it wasn't Amy in the back, but a newborn, wrapped tightly in a blanket.

Take it easy, Robert, Helen said, sensing his anger and frustration. *This isn't Wendy, and you shouldn't treat her like she is.*

Helen was right, of course, but Robert was having a hard time shutting down his anger. It seemed that at every turn there was an obstacle, something fantastic in his path that prevented him from living any semblance of a normal life.

With a deep breath, he turned his back to Cal and Aiden, and spoke directly to Shelly, deciding to take a more direct approach.

"Please, Shel, I know that you want to help, and we could definitely use your help if we go forward with this plan. But you're pregnant, and you need to think about the baby."

Shelly pressed her lips together.

"I *am* thinking about the baby, Rob. I'm thinking about what happens if you three dicks fuck up and Carson unleashes hell on Earth. Is that the kind of world you want your child being brought up into? Ask yourself that question, then decide whether or not I'm being selfish."

Robert gritted his teeth in frustration.

"Fuck," he grumbled.

Let it go for now, Rob. Let it go, and deal with it later.

Seeing that there was no way that he could win this battle, he threw his hands up in defeat. Only then did he realize the extent of his anger; he must have been clenching his fists, as the white bandage on his nub of an index finger had turned bright red.

"Fine! Just fucking great. A fucking dead guy, a pregnant woman, and me and Cal to take on Satan and his fucking minions. Sounds good to me. So how about one of you guys fill me in on this master plan of yours, then?"

Aiden spoke for the first time in a while.

"It doesn't have to be the four of us. I can get us at least one more."

Cal sucked his teeth.

"I don't know about that. I don't know if I'm comfortable bringing someone else into this mess."

Aiden made a face.

"This ain't no schoolboy, Cal. You needed worry about him—he's solid."

"Fine, four of us, then. So Shelly can stay home."

"Robbo..."

Robert thought about Helen, her quiddity trapped inside his mind, then his thoughts flicked to Allan.

He swallowed hard.

"Cal's right. No more people."

Aiden looked like he was about to protest, but instead nodded his head.

"Okay, then. But in order for our plan to work, we first have to figure out where they're holed up. Maybe that's something you can help with, Robert."

Robert frowned, the anger flooding back again.

Been feeling strange lately? Doing things that you wouldn't normally do? Getting angry a lot, Robbo?

"Me? How the fuck can I do that? I have no idea where these people are. I only went where Sean..."

He let his sentence trail off when Cal nodded at the mention of the man's name and shot a look at Aiden.

"No, no way. I'm not reaching out to him. Besides, I couldn't find him if I wanted to. He always came to me."

"And when did he come and see you?" Aiden asked.

"When the bastard needed my help, he just showed up. He came first when he needed help cleansing the Estate, then when the hospital was being overrun. Then again at Seaforth, but you know all about that one."

"Yeah, well, maybe all I have to do is hang around here, and he'll show up."

Robert mulled that over for a moment.

Maybe. Maybe Sean would detect the quiddity and show up, eventually. But he couldn't wait for *eventually.*

"But maybe it would be better if we were proactive. After all, he has something that you want, doesn't he?" Aiden said, as if he were the one inside his head reading his thoughts instead of Helen.

"What does he have, Rob?" Shelly asked.

Robert ignored her.

"Yeah, no thanks to you."

Aiden shrugged, as if the horrible ordeal that he had put Robert through back at Callahan's church was just an afterthought. In a way, Robert supposed it was, given what had happened at the Estate afterward.

Aiden suddenly snapped his fingers, a strange, hollow sound that, like the rest of him, wasn't quite *real.*

"You know what? I have a better idea. Instead of getting Sean to come to us, why don't we go see him?"

"Wait, you know where he lives?" Shelly asked, incredulous.

Aiden shook his head.

"No, but I have a number I can call him at. He usually picks a spot for us to meet."

Robert squinted at the quiddity across from him. Even though he was faded, and the light bounced strangely off of him, he somehow seemed more real than he had been back in the helicopter or at Seaforth. As if back then he had been inhibited, and his death had somehow freed him.

Robert didn't know if Aiden could actually contact Sean, or even if he wanted him to. Just thinking about the man put a sour taste in his mouth.

Leland's words suddenly echoed in his head as a soundtrack to the images of Sean at Seaforth, shooting the bound man in the head.

You look at me with such disgust, disdain, leaving me to wonder if you look at him the same way?

Both men had played him, it seemed, and Robert got the nagging suspicion that he was but a pawn in their longstanding game.

A game he'd never wanted to play, and yet one he was determined to win nonetheless.

Yeah, we'll find that bastard Sean, and this time he's going to answer all of my questions.

His eyes darted to Aiden, and he wondered how Sean would react to seeing his hired gun like this, given that he had been so opposed to even Robert touching him after Leland had grabbed his calf.

Or us, Robert, Helen reminded him. *How he'll react to us. If this guy has all this experience, he might be able to see me, too.*

Robert chewed the inside of his lip. Helen had a point.

But in the end, he had no choice. He had to find Carson, he had to find the book, and for fuck's sake, he had to get Amy back.

Robert plopped himself down on the chair and shook his head.

"Make the call, Aiden. Just make the call before I change my mind."

Chapter 9

"STOP THE TAPE—REWIND."

Hugh did as he was told, and Ed leaned in close.

"Roll forward, slow—*slow*."

He paid close attention to Michael as he entered the frame.

"There! You see that?"

Hugh moved his face to within inches of the screen.

"See what? That's our guy, our resident cannibal psychopath. What about him?"

Ed finished his third Coke in one big gulp. Then he brought a fist to his chest and let out a small burp.

"You know why they call us 'detectives,' Hugh?"

"I guess—"

"No, no guessing. It's because we *detect* things, get it?"

Hugh turned on his swivel chair and glared at Ed.

"Only thing I'm detecting right now is my increased blood pressure."

Ed laughed. This was a side of Hugh that he hadn't seen before—sarcastic, funny. Raw.

He liked it.

"Just watch the tape, Hugh. Rewind it once more."

Hugh threw his hands up, but did as he was instructed.

"Aaaaaaaand, right there," Ed said, his voice brimming with pretension.

"Hmm. He said something."

Ed mock clapped.

"Bravo! He *did* say something, but more importantly, he said something to *someone*. And this Michael cat doesn't strike me as the type of person who makes small talk with a random stranger, does he?"

Hugh shrugged.

"No, but he could just be talking to himself…he's a bit of a strange one, this Michael. After all, he does eat people, lest we forget."

Ed held up a finger.

"Or, smartass, the woman in the park is right, and our pal was with two other people."

Hugh let the tape play. On the video, Michael looked much like the woman with Tootsie had told them, offering her story even more credence: his hair was messy, his tie loose, and the top button of his shirt was undone. The camera wasn't HD, and he couldn't be sure, but Ed thought that the man was sweating. The rest of the video was uneventful, and showed most of what the ATM video showed. Michael simply walked up to the machine, put his card in, took out some money, and then left the way he had come, vanishing out of frame.

When the video had first surfaced, PD's initial reaction had been to shut off Michael's bank accounts and flag his cards. The theory was simple: cut off his money supply and cross your fingers, hope that he did something stupid that would give him away.

Problem was, Michael was anything but stupid.

It went without saying that Ed had very much been opposed to this idea, despite the obvious flight risk that the man posed. The man was an egomaniac, *had* to be an egomaniac, and the longer he went without knowing that they were after him, the better. Besides, Michael Young had netted 1.2 mil last year, and yet the subpoenas of his bank accounts had revealed a paltry combined balance of 323k. There was a lot of cheddar that wasn't accounted for, and Michael didn't seem to Ed like the kind of man that spent frivolously, or gambled, or blew his wad on a pound of coke.

Nope, the man had different, and decidedly cheaper extra-curriculars. If they cut off his cash supply, he would just use his other accounts that they couldn't trace.

"What're you thinking, Ed?"

Ed shook his head.

"I'm thinking that there is no way that Michael is going to use this card again."

Hugh gave him a look, but Ed ignored it.

"Let's look at another camera, then. Only now we have three people to spy on and not just one. Maybe we'll get lucky; maybe Michael went inside high-fiving his co-conspirators and grabbed a bag of Cheetos and our mustachioed friend out there just forgot. *What you thinking*, Hugh?"

Hugh rolled his eyes.

"I think you better get yourself a Diet Coke this time, because this here is a lot of material to go through."

***

Hugh was right, it took them three hours to go through every one of the tapes for Tuesday. Ed counted eight people that came and went into or around the gas station sandwiching the hour that Michael was at the ATM.

Two of them stood out to him: a woman and two bald men.

"Well, which one should we focus on, Hugh?"

Hugh made a face, but answered immediately.

"The woman is out, doesn't matter how sketchy she looks. The woman in the park was clear about Michael being with two men. No sign of a skinny fucker with non-smiling eyes, either. So that leaves the two bald men."

Hugh fiddled with the video, bringing up the image of a round man in a beater barging through the door. He scratched his nuts through a pair of stained sweatpants, then made his way to the cash. He was wearing a 'Make America Great Again' mesh cap, and when Mr. Edmonds looked down to get his change, the man flipped the bird to the camera.

Ed shook his head.

What the hell is this world coming to?

"This guy is a real treat, that much is clear."

"And the other one?"

Hugh quickly switched tapes and ran the other recording. This one was timestamped seventeen minutes after Michael first walked up to the ATM.

The video was from outside the building, and the sun flared on the lens, washing out the image. Still, Ed could clearly make out the silhouette of an overweight man, short and bald, waddling toward the bathroom around the side. He pulled the bathroom door open, blocking out the sun for a split second, then disappeared inside. Four minutes later, he came out again and left the way he had come.

"Then there's this guy," Hugh said. "Doesn't say or do anything offensive, just goes into the shitter and either rubs one out or takes a dump and then leaves. Doesn't buy gas, though."

Ed nodded.

"Which one is our guy, Hugh? Number one Republican or Hairy Palms McGee?"

Hugh chortled.

"Jesus, I feel like Miss Marple here."

"Talk it out, talk it out."

Hugh rolled his eyes.

"Now I feel like one of those fucking losers on Who Wants To Be A Millionaire. Is this a trick question? Did you see a candlestick in one of their hands? Mr. Mustard in the dining room with the waffle maker? C'mon, Ed. I'm tired, my eyes hurt, my *ass* hurts. Just tell me what you see."

Ed made a face.

"I'll give you a hint. Roll back this tape to when he opens the door and it blocks out the sun—limits the flare on the lens."

Hugh jogged the tape to the appropriate spot.

"What do you see?"

And that's frustration, Baby Hughey. Keep it in check.

And thankfully, Hugh somehow managed. For all of his sarcastic remarks, Hugh seemed generally interested in learning.

After a moment of keen observation, Hugh said, "I see a fat man in a shirt two sizes too small and—" He stopped mid-sentence and jogged the tape back a quarter second. Then he broke into a smile. "Shit, I'll be damned. I see a t-shirt with Mickey fucking Mouse on it."

"*And the fat man was wearing a Disney t-shirt*," Ed said in his best impression of the woman with the multiple rhinoplasty surgeries. "Snap a pic, send it to Mac back at the station. See if anyone recognizes him, run it through the police recognition database and all that fancy stuff."

Hugh, still staring at the screen, pulled his cell phone out and snapped a pic. Then he clicked madly on the tiny keyboard before putting it back in his pocket.

"I'll be damned, Ed; the Nose is working well today. *Thar* be some mighty fine detective work," he added out of the corner of his mouth, accompanied by an exaggerated fist pump. "What now, ossifer?"

Ed collected his cans of Coke and prepared to leave.

"Now, my good man, we *detect*; detectives *detect*, Hugh. Let that be your first lesson of the day."

Hugh laughed and stood.

"First? Is this my first lesson, Pope Pius?"

Chapter 10

"NO, NOT HERE—WE can't meet here."

Rob, Cal, and Shelly were all crouched in the Harlop sitting room, the former two sipping on scotch, eyes wide and ears perked.

All of them were holding their breath.

Sean had picked up on the fifth ring, just as Aiden had said he would.

The sound of Sean's voice through the tinny cell speaker brought back deep-rooted feelings of anger and disgust in Robert. The man was a self-serving asshole who had put Cal and Shelly and Allan at risk, using them as a ploy to get Robert to do his bidding. And that said nothing of the shit that he had put him through at the church.

Aiden wasn't to blame for that; at least, he wasn't *all* to blame. But he wasn't blameless, either.

But what could he do to a man that was already dead?

I'm going to do more than get the fucking book back from you, Sean. That's a promise.

"And Robert? He's fine?"

Even this question made him seethe—not even a whisper of a mention of any of the others. To Sean, they didn't matter. To Sean, only Robert, the son of Leland Black, mattered in their fucking game.

Rook meet pawn.

"He's fine. The rest are fine, too."

"Anything happen?"

Aiden hesitated, and Robert cringed, thinking that the man had given himself away.

"No. All clear."

"You sure?"

"Sure."

Now it was Sean's turn to pause.

"Yeah, we should meet."

"Agreed."

Sean proceeded to give Aiden an address Robert didn't recognize, and he quickly looked to Cal, who was already on his phone, looking it up.

"Can you be at the Tower by eight?"

The question clearly took Aiden by surprise.

"Tonight?"

"Tonight."

Robert checked his watch. Their discussions had taken them well into the morning hours, and his watch read a quarter to five in the morning. Just seeing those numbers made his eyelids droop. On instinct, he looked over to Shelly, who looked even worse for wear.

Four months pregnant...she shouldn't be up this late.

He could feel Helen cringe at this, as if reminding him, for what felt like the hundredth time, that Shelly was a grown woman who was perfectly capable of making her own decisions. While Robert agreed in principle, he wasn't sure that she was qualified to make the right ones.

Especially given her history at the church, a card that Robert still held close to his chest.

"Eight. I'll be there."

"Good. Meet me out back. I have another job for you."

Aiden went to click *END* on the phone, but Cal hopped to his feet and slipped it away from him before he touched it, while at the same time being careful not to come in contact with Aiden himself.

They had used Cal's phone, unsure of how or if Aiden's would work, which was an option only because they were both burners, like the one that Robert had used back at the church.

They sat in silence for about a minute before Cal yawned loudly.

"I need some sleep."

"Me too," Shelly said, struggling to get to her feet. Her belly was more than just thick, Robert realized. With her standing the way she was, he thought he saw a roundness there, a burgeoning pregnant belly waiting to be born, and he almost smiled.

Almost.

The truth was, he wasn't sure how to feel about this whole pregnancy, or if he had even fully come to terms with it.

It seemed wrong, similar to the way that it had felt wrong sleeping with Shelly in the first place.

Like he was cheating on Amy and Wendy.

Wendy's dead, Helen reminded him, and Robert grimaced, trying to shut her off, to keep her out of his most private of thoughts.

When he had first drawn the woman's quiddity inside him, she had been confined to her own space, a dull pressure localized to the left side of his head. But now that she seemed to have grown more comfortable, she appeared to be everywhere, pervading his neurons like a wayward electrical impulse. And having someone, dead or alive, capable of perusing his very thoughts, his memories, his feelings, as they happened was more than a little disconcerting.

Still, Helen occasionally offered a nugget of wisdom that he wouldn't have come up with on his own.

Occasionally.

Even thinking about this now made him uncomfortable, knowing that she could, and probably was, listening in. As unnerving as it was, he thought he could put up with it for now.

He would figure out how to send Helen on her way eventually. He just hoped that the process was buried somewhere in the book.

He had promised.

And then there was the issue of Shelly, and the fact that, like he, she had been at the church with Father Callahan.

As if she was also in his head, Shelly turned toward him in that instant.

"You coming?"

Robert reached into his pocket and felt the hard corner of the picture of Shelly as a child. It was strange, as the last time he had done this very same thing, it had been with a picture of Amy.

Fuck, I miss you, Amy. I'm going to get you back, I promise.

"Yeah, I'm coming," he said softly. And then he went to her and wrapped an arm around her waist and together they headed upstairs.

On their way, he heard Cal ask Aiden what he was going to do.

"I mean, do quiddity need to sleep?"

There was no answer.

"And that gun, what's it shoot? Ghost bullets?"

Unsurprisingly, Aiden didn't answer this query either.

Cal said something else, but Shelly and Robert were already so far up the stairs that he couldn't make out the words.

Within minutes, they were both lying on their backs, snoring.

Chapter 11

"MAN, IF YOU WOULD only just tell me what you're looking for, maybe I can help."

Ed hadn't answered the question the first time Hugh had asked it, and he wasn't about to answer it this time, either.

Detect, detect, detect. Detectives detect, Hugh.

"Turn here," he instructed.

Hugh hesitated.

"What are you waiting for?" Ed asked. Now he was becoming annoyed. He hated giving up the driving, but it was the only way he could stare out the window the entire time.

"You said turn, Ed. This is an intersection—sorry, but I don't have your Nose."

Ed stared at his partner.

"What?"

"Which way? Which way do you want me to turn, Ed?"

Ed looked right, then left, realizing that he hadn't picked this street for any particular reason, only that he was getting bored of driving straight.

It was well into the evening now, and they had already been to more than two dozen different bars, strip joints, seedy gambling joints, you name it, in suburban NYC. Just the thought of some of these places made Ed feel dirty, inside and out.

Their efforts, rather predictably, had led them nowhere. Ed knew that it was a wild goose chase, but it wasn't completely unfounded. After Hugh had sent Mac the picture back at the station, the man had pinged Ed to see what was up. And then he had whispered a little nugget in Ed's ear: one of Michael's accounts from a smaller bank had pinged that same Tuesday. Another withdrawal had been made from an ATM, an older one that hadn't been retrofitted with a camera just yet. The PD had done their diligence, but they hadn't come up with anything.

But they had been looking for a man in a suit, not a man in a Mickey shirt.

Still, a wild goose chase, that was for sure.

In the very least, it was a way to kill time, a way to get to know this Hugh Freeman fella a little better.

"Right," he said at last, just because it seemed *right*.

Hugh said nothing, but turned nonetheless. If the man had been on his final nerve back at the gas station, he was a live wire now.

"Hugh, you know why—wait! Wait, stop here."

"Here? There's no—"

"Stop! Stop the car!"

The car jarred as it bumped up onto the curb, and Ed swore.

"Really?" he said, turning to Hugh.

Hugh shrugged and put the car into park.

"What? You fucking shouted for me to stop like there was a purse snatcher on the prowl."

Ed shook his head and flicked his eyes out the window. The car was parked directly outside a bar with glowing neon lights that read: *Panty Snatcher*.

"Classy joint. This your kind of spot, Ed?"

***

"Beer," Ed said.

The bartender stopped cleaning a glass and looked over at him.

"Bud or Coors?"

"Coors."

Before getting his order, the bartender turned to Hugh, all the while rubbing the inside of a pint glass with a filthy dish towel.

"You?"

"Beer's fine."

The bartender sighed.

"What kind of beer?"

Ed didn't care for the man's attitude.

"Coors."

The bartender nodded, then, unbelievably, took another two minutes to finish "cleaning" the glass before he fetched their beers. When he slid them on the table, he stood there, staring at them.

"Yes?" Ed asked, confused and annoyed by this whole ordeal. This was to be their last bar of the day before heading back to the station, so deciding to have a beer instead of just coming out and asking about Michael or the other guy felt like the thing to do. But Ed was quickly starting to regret the decision.

"Three fifty."

Ed stared at the man.

"Plus tip."

Hugh spoke up before Ed lashed out at the man.

"If you want to get paid, shoot us the bill."

The bartender pressed his lips together.

"No bill. Cash only."

"What do you mean, no bill? You have—"

Ed reached over and touched his partner's arm, quieting him. Then he calmly took a sip of his beer. It was flat. He went to his pocket next, but instead of grabbing his wallet, he pulled his detective shield and laid it on the bar.

This wasn't the time for Hugh's tact and charm. It was too late, and he was too tired for that.

The bartender's already sour expression turned into something akin to disgust at the sight of the shield.

"Listen, buddy, forget the bill for now, would you?"

His eyes narrowed.

"What do you want?"

Ed took a deep breath. Unlike with the woman in the park, dealing with surly NYC suburbanites was his domain.

"We're looking for two men."

The bartender, still frowning, held out his hand and made a 'gimme' gesture.

Ed turned to Hugh and indicated for him to hand over his phone with the image of the man from the gas station security footage, while at the same time, he pulled the photograph from Michael's work ID out of his pocket.

The man took a cursory glance at the phone first, then the photograph.

"Never seen either of them," he said with a shrug.

Ed had stared at his face the entire time, knowing the man was going to answer the exact way he had, no matter what question they asked. But he didn't twitch, didn't seem fazed by either photo.

He was telling the truth.

Ed looked around. It was a shitty bar, one of the worst that they had been to today. Dimly lit, the bar itself was a dinged-up piece of wood that he expected was barely a sliver of a grade above plywood, and the stools upon which he and Hugh sat, two of only six, felt like they were fashioned out of cinderblocks. Behind them were a handful of booths covered in what looked like cracked and torn leather, but was much more likely some synthetic variant, and the walls were covered in peeling beige wallpaper.

Ed couldn't tell if there was a pattern on the paper, or if the markings were just random stains. If he were a betting man, he would have put his pension on the latter. But of all of these attractions, it was the neon 'u' of a Budweiser sign that drew his attention. Or, more specifically, it was the small black eye embedded inside it that he found interesting.

If the man had just been polite, shown a modicum of respect, Ed would have left it at that. But he hadn't.

He was a dick.

"We're going to have to see your camera footage," he said simply, choking down a massive gulp of the warm, flat beer.

The man's response was immediate, but unlike before when questioned about the two men, he looked away as he spoke.

"Don't work."

"I think it does, bud," Ed replied. "Look, I don't want anything to do with you, this shitty bar, or this—" He picked up what was left of the beer and sloshed it in the glass. "—or this terrible beer. We are investigating a homicide, several homicides, and I need to see footage from two Tuesdays ago. That's it. Don't care about anything else."

The man crossed his arms over his narrow chest.

"Don't work."

Ed turned to Hugh and offered him a look. Then he turned back to the bartender and in one motion, he knocked his beer over the bar.

"What—?"

When the man moved to pick up the glass, Ed reached over and grabbed his arm and pulled him close. The beer dripped off the other side of the bar and soaked the front of the bartender's shirt and pants.

"The camera fucking works, bud. Now get me that footage before I get my buddy from the IRS to come in and check your books, how 'bout that?"

The man was shaking in Ed's grip, which gave him pause. A man like this, in the *Panty Snatcher* of all places, must have come across many an unsavory character in his time. In fact, based on the crude tattoos that marked his forearms, the man himself likely had a shady past of his own.

And yet grabbing his wrist the way Ed was now had struck fear directly into his heart.

Maybe this isn't such a wild goose chase, after all.

Chapter 12

"**WHAT DO YOU REMEMBER** about your childhood, Shel?"

Robert was lying in bed beside her, his hand tracing a circle on her belly. They had slept until noon, and they would have slept for even longer had the sun not been blazing in through the single window in the room.

The question caught Shelly off guard, and she turned on her side, away from him. His fingers tickled her pale back gently.

"Why do you ask?"

Robert shrugged, trying to sound natural.

"I dunno, was just thinking…we're going to have a child together, and yet I realize that I know next to nothing about you."

Shelly rolled over again, her expression severe.

"You know everything about me, Rob. It doesn't matter where I was born, who I was raised by—what matters is who I am now, and that you know—and that should be enough."

Robert squinted at her. His question had been innocuous enough, and yet her reaction didn't match it.

He probed a little harder.

"I didn't mean anything by it. Just wanted to know where you were born, what your childhood was like. You never speak of your parents. I mean, is this baby going to have grandparents? That's a reasonable question, isn't it?"

Robert detected a hint of sadness in her features, but it faded quickly.

"All you need to know, Robert, is that we are going to be good—*great*—parents to the child in my belly. That's all that matters. If, of course, you stop treating *me* like a child."

Robert ignored the comment and stared, trying to figure out if Shelly was either lying to protect her secret of being at the church or if, like him, she was embarrassed by not being able to remember her childhood.

"Why the fuck are you staring at me like that?"

She doesn't remember, Helen said with conviction. *She's acting this way because she doesn't remember.*

"Sorry, just don't know why you are getting so upset," he grumbled.

Shelly sighed.

"No, I'm sorry. It's just—it's been a fucked-up two days, Robert. I didn't mean to be short with you. Things are...well, fucked up."

She leaned over and kissed him on the lips.

"But enough about me; it's not like there's anything going on with my body, hormones and all that. You know, a fetus sapping my strength, stealing my food." She smiled a weak smile. "How are you? How's the hand? The scrape? The ankle?"

Robert shrugged. To be honest, he hadn't actually thought about his injuries since he had awoken.

With a groan, he slipped the covers off and pulled himself into a seated position.

He hadn't thought about them until now, that is. The scrape on his chest was not as bad as he had initially thought, and even though the gauze that Shelly had placed over it was peeling back in some places, it seemed to have stopped bleeding. It was going to leave a nasty scar, but that was about it—no permanent damage there. A quick roll of his ankle revealed a limited range of motion, but he doubted it was broken.

That left his ear and his finger.

His ear had lost a small chunk from the top where the bullet had grazed him, but it was just an ear and he could still hear just fine.

His finger, on the other hand...

Robert brought the mangled digit up to his face and examined the crude wrapping that had long since turned a deep crimson. The sight of it ending long before it should have was bizarre, and Robert instinctively tried to bend it.

It was a mistake he soon regretted, and it was all he could do not to cry out.

"Fuck!"

Shelly was upright in an instant, moving fluidly despite her new figure.

Robert stared as the cloth started to get more and more wet as new blood soaked the cloth. Pain shot up his arm.

"Gonna need to stitch that up, Rob," Shelly informed him softly.

Robert shook his head as he straightened his finger once more. Reluctantly, the nub went back to its original position.

"No time."

"You're gonna lose more than your fucking finger if you don't take care of it."

"Can you get a bowl of warm water, some towels, disinfectant, and some Super Glue?"

Shelly made a face.

"What the fuck do I look like? A pharmacy?"

Robert couldn't bring himself to smile. Instead, he just shook his head.

"It's under the sink. I put it there when Amy was—when Amy—Amy—"

Shelly wrapped her arms around him and held him tight. Just mentioning her name had become a challenge now, as he imagined Leland gripping her shoulders, his horrible face staring down at her.

And the Goat...the Goat is coming...

Robert shuddered, and then composed himself.

"I put some first-aid supplies under the sink when we first moved in. Maybe you can grab it for me? I think I put some glue in there, too. We can stick it together, hopefully that'll keep the swelling down and stop the bleeding. There's some ibuprofen in there, too—could use maybe two dozen of those, as well."

"Sure," Shelly said, and stood.

At some time during the night—or morning, by the time they had actually gone to bed—she had removed all of her clothes, and as she made her way to the bathroom to collect the supplies, he marveled at her body.

Even with her growing belly, he found her nearly irresistible, the extra meat in her thighs and ass looking even more beautiful to him now.

And so very different than Wendy.

The thought had come out of nowhere, but that didn't make it any less true. Where Wendy had been thin and wiry, all angles, Shelly was curvy.

As he watched her ass as she made it to the bathroom, and despite everything, he felt the front of his boxers start to tighten.

Just outside the bathroom door, Shelly half turned and looked back at him.

"You fucking perv," she said with a laugh. "Ogling a pregnant woman. Fetish much?"

Robert blushed.

In a way, her response was a relief. No matter how much things had changed over the past six months or so, it was good to have some constants, something reliable.

Something real.

***

It was bad; really bad. So bad, in fact, that once Robert caught sight of the gleaming white bone poking up through the ground beef-looking skin where Michael's teeth had gnawed it off, he had to look away.

"Oh God...just get it over with," he said through gritted teeth. Shelly worked quickly, first cleaning the wound and then applying the antiseptic lotion. But it quickly became clear that she was out of her depth. She would make a great mother, cleaning out scraped knees and dealing with minor cuts, but she was ill-prepared for cannibal wounds.

In fact, the bite was so ragged that Robert's initial plan to glue the nub wasn't going to work. There just wasn't enough skin left to cover the exposed bone—he needed a skin graft, and they both knew it.

"Robert, you have to go to the hospital—you need to get this fixed. And you need broad-spectrum antibiotics—who knows what kind of bacteria that guy, that fucking *freak*, has in his system. You've gotta take care of this now."

Robert's eyes flicked to her face, then her stomach.

There was no way in Hell—no way in the Marrow—he was going to let her come with them to see Sean, let alone to confront Carson.

And with this realization, a plan began to form in his mind.

"You're right. And these"—he shook the bottle of Advil in his other hand—"aren't going to cut it for much longer."

It was always best to sprinkle truth on top of lies. Like when he had been staring at Jonah's burning corpse, this callousness saddened him.

But it didn't change his mind. He had lost one wife and child; he wasn't about to lose more people he loved.

Shelly's shoulders sagged with relief. Encouraged by her response, he started nodding and continued, "I'll going to the hospital, see if they can fix me up quick."

Shelly's posture changed again.

"A quick fix? You think that this is a quick fix?"

"Probably not," he admitted. "But I can't leave it like this."

"And the meeting with Sean? What about that?"

Robert tried his best to look dejected.

"I dunno. I'll tell Aiden to call Sean back, tell him that something came up."

Shelly looked dubious.

"Something came up? Sean's really gonna buy that?"

"Fuck, I don't know, Shelly, I just—*arrgh*—"

He grabbed the wrist of his injured hand and bent at the waist.

"—it fucking kills..."

Shelly shot to her feet.

"Yeah, we're going to the hospital, all right. Let me just—"

Robert stared at her belly, at the dirt that covered her skin.

"Go have a quick shower, clean yourself off first and I'll go tell Aiden and Cal. Get them to call Sean."

Shelly stared at him for a moment, and he could literally see her gears turning.

She's not buying it, Helen thought. *She knows you're lying.*

But for once, Helen was wrong. Shelly nodded, then reached over and grabbed the gauze from the basket. Then, as gingerly as possible, she wrapped it loosely over the exposed bone and glistening flesh.

"Put this on it for now."

With that, she rose and headed to the shower.

"I'll be down in ten," she said, running her hand through her short blonde hair. When her fingers snagged, she corrected herself, "Make that fifteen."

Robert smiled as he watched her go. When she closed the door, his face went slack.

"I'm sorry, Shelly," he whispered as he stood and quickly dressed. "But I just can't risk it."

As he put the bottle of Advil in his pocket, his fingers brushed the hard corner of a photograph.

Chapter 13

GRABBING THE BARTENDER'S ARM had snapped his tough veneer. That simple act, disregarding, of course, that Ed had technically assaulted the man, was arguably the best piece of 'policework' of the day: the man had veritably opened up like a leaking dam, and now he wouldn't shut up.

The bartender described in great detail a man who had come in here, sat down beside one of the regulars, ordered some tequila shots, and then, without warning, grabbed his arm much like Ed had a moment ago.

"It's not the first time some guy grabbed me across the bar, and it won't be the last, but this was different...it was his eyes..."

The bartender went on to describe them as cold, dead eyes, along with three dozen other adjectives, and Ed was instantly reminded of what the woman in the park had told them.

His eyes definitely weren't smiling.

"I think he would have cut me up right then and there, sliced and diced me without a second thought."

Ed nodded, and Hugh shot him a glance.

It appeared as if they might have gotten lucky after all.

There are no coincidences.

It looked like they might have caught their goose.

"The video camera is a simple feed, works on VHS," the bartender said as he took them to the kitchen. "Records right here."

"Jesus, what's with these archaic security systems today?" Hugh muttered. But the way he lifted up a filthy pot, Ed wasn't sure if the man was more surprised by the equipment or the fact that the *Panty Snatcher* actually had a kitchen.

"What?"

"Nothing."

The man pulled a key out of his pocket and opened the drawer beneath the TV/VCR combo unit that sat beside a couple of kegs of beer.

"I usually only keep the footage for a few days—tapes are expensive, you know, and there's no point in keeping this shit if ain't nothin' happened."

Ed nodded.

"But something *did* happen last Tuesday, so you kept it."

"Yep."

He pulled out the tape—unlabeled, Ed noted—and put it into the unit. It whirred and remained dark for a moment, but then the monitor flicked on. The bartender fast-forwarded a couple of hours, but when a dark-haired woman in a tight leather outfit sat down and ordered a drink, Ed asked him to play it in real time.

"Any audio on this?"

The bartender shook his head.

"Who's this?" Hugh asked, tapping the back of the woman's head on the screen.

"A regular, comes in at least once a week. Never says a word; men come up to her all the time and hit on her, but she just brushes them off. Pretty gal like that, you'd think this isn't the place for her. But I'm thinking she fits right in, if you know what I mean."

A man suddenly walked into the shot, a thin man with short black stubble on his recently shaved head.

"She never says a word; until today, that is."

Hugh hushed him, for which Ed was grateful. The man's ramblings had quickly gone from helpful to annoying.

In the video, the man walked directly up to the bar and took up residence beside the woman. He seemed to be leaning away from her at first, and then he ordered a drink, and their incredibly cheery neighborhood bartender served him after a short delay. Then the man reached for the woman. She turned and instantly dropped her glass, a mixture of shock and recognition forming on her pale face. The man took several minutes trying to convince her of something, but she was having none of it.

And then the altercation with the bartender came next, just as he had described it, with the addition of spilled tequila.

For a split second, the man at the bar's eyes flicked upward and he appeared to stare into the camera. And then the image exploded into static, and Ed instinctively pulled away from the monitor.

"Stays like this until about three minutes after they left—no idea what happened. They chatted, kissed, then took off," the bartender managed, his voice sounding constricted.

The video alone was enough to bring back the feelings of fear in him.

"Go back," Ed instructed. "Go back to where he looked up at the camera."

The man pressed the rewind button and backed up the tape.

"There. Stop there."

The man on the screen was pretty much the way the woman at the park had described him: thin, bordering on sickly, with gray-colored skin and sunken cheeks. His head had been shaved recently, maybe a couple of weeks ago, but was now showing signs of growing back.

But it was his eyes that convinced Ed that this was their guy. His eyes weren't cold and dead like Michael's, or even crazy like the guy in the Mickey Mouse t-shirt; rather, these were *alive*. Dancing, flickering without light, excited like a child on Christmas morning.

But, paradoxically, they were also soulless pits that Ed felt he could get lost in by staring too long.

He shook his head, trying to shake the strange feelings that threatened to overcome him.

"This is our guy," he whispered more to himself than to anyone else. Hugh surprised him by answering.

"Yep, that's him. That's *definitely* him."

"Take a picture, Hugh." Then, to the bartender, he added, "Anything else you can tell me about these two?"

The man seemed to mull the question over for a moment. After seeing the man onscreen, he'd apparently suddenly decided that maybe it was best to slow his wagging tongue.

Fear could do that to a man.

Ed prodded a little deeper.

"I'm not asking for Social Security numbers and credit cards here. Help us out." When these appeals failed to break his stern expression, Ed tried a different tactic. "Look at it this way: you tell us something that helps us get this guy, and you won't have to ever risk seeing him in your classy establishment ever again. And when we bring him in, I'll forget all about the little story you just told us; about how, oh, maybe you *didn't* rat him out."

The man grimaced, realizing now that he had been played. He had no choice but to offer up any information he had.

"The guy mentioned something about being in prison, out on parole, and the woman called him Carson, I think."

Ed nodded, locking these facts away in his brain.

Hugh leaned forward and tapped the back of the woman's head.

"You said the woman's a regular? Any info on her?"

The bartender shook his head.

"No, like I said, she never says much. Her name is Bella, but that's all I know."

"Take a few more pics, Hugh."

As the man snapped away, Ed turned to the bartender.

"We're gonna need the tape—you don't mind, do you?"

The man shrugged, and looked almost relieved at the thought of getting rid of it, of putting the entire encounter behind him.

"Whatever."

"We're good here," Hugh said.

"Send the pics to Mac, see if he can come up with anything. Let him know about the name Carson and to check prison databases."

The bartender pressed eject, and when he went to go grab the tape, Ed reached for it. The man recoiled, clearly fearing that he would be grabbed again.

Ed smirked and took the tape.

"C'mon, Hugh, let's head back to the station. Thanks for the help, bud. And thanks for the beer," he added as he turned and left with Hugh in tow.

"That'll be three fifty each!" the bartender hollered after them.

Without turning, Ed said, "I think your beer's gone bad. Better get that checked before the inspector comes through."

As Ed passed the two kegs, he reached out and yanked the tubing from the one nearest him, and beer started to spray onto the floor behind them.

"Fuck! What the fuck!"

Chapter 14

"**You fucking sure about** this, Robbo?"

Robert opened the car door while shaking his head. The familiarity of his car was oddly soothing to him. In a completely foreign world, it was nice to have something from the time before.

This was only after he disregarded the emotions that came with the realization that it had been stolen from him in South Carolina, and the only reason he had gotten it back was because Aiden had told him where he had parked it.

"No," he added, before stepping inside. "I'm not sure of any of this."

"I mean about Shelly."

Robert sat in the driver's seat and shut the door. He waited for Aiden to climb into the back, and Cal into the front, before answering.

"I told you, she had some morning sickness. Was feeling awful. She'll be fine—she'll come with us when we go get Carson," he lied. "Let's get a fucking move on."

Cal closed the door, and Robert glanced up at him in the rearview mirror.

His friend's expression was one of such disbelief that, had the situation been different, Robert might have laughed. Cal knew he was lying—he knew *Shelly*, after all—but for some reason, he refrained from calling him on it. Maybe Cal had come to his senses and realized that what they were about to do should not—*could not*—involve a pregnant woman, for Christ's sake.

It didn't matter his motivations. What mattered was that they had less than an hour before they had to meet Sean, and Shelly would be safe here back at the Estate.

For some reason, despite what happened here yesterday, he knew this last part to be true.

Robert put the car into drive and rolled around the statue, and pulled up to the gate.

"You wanna open it, Cal?"

Cal hopped out without a word, and Robert glanced nervously in the rearview mirror, waiting with bated breath. The horrible screeching of the gate opening drew him back. Out of all the things wrong with the Harlop Estate, he hated the gate the most. No matter what the hell they did—grease it, lube it, replace the gears—it remained an obstinate piece of wrought iron that was like a physical pain in his side.

Robert leaned out the window.

"C'mon, Cal, I can fit through. Let's go!"

Cal hurried back and jumped into the passenger seat. Before he had even closed the door, Robert peeled out of the driveway.

Despite his best efforts, he couldn't resist the urge to glance in the rearview one final time.

The Estate door was suddenly thrown wide and a familiar figure with a round belly stood in the entrance, hands on her hips. The car jostled and a scraping sound filled the evening air.

"Fuck," Cal grumbled.

By looking in the mirror, Robert had veered to the right and scraped the passenger side door on the gate.

"Let's get the fuck out of here," Robert said before any of them could change their mind.

***

"I feel like a fucking child," Cal said absently after they had been driving for about an hour.

"How do you mean?"

"Well, you know how a child will, like, burn their hand on the stove, and then do it again and again?"

Robert thought of Amy, how sweet she was, how much she liked to draw. He recalled the incredibly detailed drawing that she had made in the bar on the day of Wendy's funeral.

It's the ocean, Daddy. I drew it for you.

Cal didn't have children, so he couldn't blame the man for being so wrong about them. They weren't helpless, mindless creatures.

They were, in fact, a lot smarter than people gave them credit. And Amy was definitely on the high end of that scale. Still, he understood what Cal was saying, despite not comprehending the context.

"What do you mean?"

Cal sighed and rubbed his eyes. Clearly, he hadn't gotten the same sort of rest that Robert and Shelly had.

"Do we have a plan? Seriously, we did the same shit at both Pinedale and Seaforth: barge in there like retarded GI commandos, minus the training." He turned to Aiden in the backseat who had acquired his typical deadpan expression. "No offense. But, Robert, what are we supposed to do this time when we meet Sean, huh? Kidnap him?"

Robert said nothing, and instead deferred to the 'retarded GI commando' for an answer. When Aiden realized that they were both waiting for him to speak, he shifted the chaw from one side of his lip to the other. In that moment, a strange thought came to Robert.

What happens when he spits? Does he have to spit?

The man's words brought about renewed focus.

"You bring the stuff I told you to? Put it in the trunk?"

Cal nodded.

"Shovel, rope, heavy bag? Jug of water? Put it all in there."

Aiden took a deep breath.

"Then, yeah, that's exactly what we're going to do. Kidnap the man. Make him talk. Make him tell us where Carson is."

"And you're sure this is going to work?" Robert asked tentatively.

Aiden reached for the empty coffee cup between the front seats, causing Robert and Cal to dramatically lean away, toward their respective doors. It was the same cup that he had used to spit in when he had held a gun to Robert's head outside Callahan's church. Aiden swirled it a bit, made a face, and then spat a thick stream of tobacco juice.

And that answers that.

"Fuck no. I'm not sure about nothin' anymore. But it's all we got."

Chapter 15

"ALRIGHTY, HUGHEY, LET ME hear what you got."

Hugh raised an eyebrow.

"*Hughey*? *What 'I got'*? Alright there, Martin Riggs."

Ed just kept on smiling, then indicated the photographs laid out on the table in front of them. It had taken a good hour to get from the *Panty Snatcher* to the precinct, despite thin traffic for a Tuesday night. Once back, they had taken up residence in the empty lunch room. Hugh had spun his magic with the computers and had managed to print out larger and seemingly better-quality images of the four suspects, who they had promptly named Larry (man in the Mickey shirt), Curly (man with the dead eyes), Mo (the girl), and Mike (Michael Young), and laid them out on the table. Mike was in the middle, with Larry and Mo on one side and Curly on the other.

"Seriously," Ed said at last when it was clear that a hypothesis from Hugh wasn't forthcoming. "What are you thinking happened to our boy Mike?"

Ed observed his new partner closely, even before he began to speak. The fact that underlying all of his sarcasm and wit Hugh genuinely liked the challenge, got a kick out of putting together these human puzzle pieces, was something to be admired.

Throughout his tenure as a detective, and as a beat cop before that, Ed had seen many different types of police officers: the macho type, the aggressive, usually short, asshole of a cop; the quiet, contemplative, insecure type; the paycheck type; and the least common, the puzzler.

Hugh was a puzzler, through and through. With a dash of the paycheck type thrown in and a sprinkling of contemplation to boot.

"I don't know, Ed. I have no idea why this guy, a wealthy Wall Street psycho"—he jabbed Mike in the nose—"would hang out with this guy." He thumbed the fatso in the Disney shirt.

"Well—"

Hugh held up his finger, stopping Ed.

"So that leaves Curly and Mo. *Huh*. They have to be the link between the two; there is no scenario I can imagine—correction, no *reasonable* scenario I can imagine—in which Michael interacts with Larry."

"Not in a past life? Childhood?"

Hugh shook his head.

"No. No way. Mike here has been keeping his devil a secret. Has been since the day he was born, I figure. Speaking to this man here, that's just a recipe to get caught."

"You saw his setup, right? The cage, the sub-basement dungeon?"

"Yep."

"Why would he leave that? What would make him give all that up? I mean, for a sick fuck like him, he seemed to be like a pig in shit."

Hugh sighed.

"We went over this already. Blackmail, death, prison."

"Can't be the latter two; we saw him on video."

"Which leaves blackmail, buuuuut..."

Ed reached forward and poured himself another two fingers of Crown Royal Northern Harvest. He wasn't fond of drinking at work, but there was no one around and it had been a long, busy day. A quick glance revealed that Hugh was still working on his drink.

He took a sip.

"Does our boy Mike look like someone susceptible to blackmail?"

Hugh grimaced.

"Maybe. Doubt it, though."

"So then why?"

Hugh grabbed his drink, finished it, and held the empty mug out for a refill. The Nose obliged.

"Don't know. I don't fucking know."

"Don't get frustrated. Let me ask you something: why does an alcoholic leave the bar?"

Hugh rolled his eyes so dramatically that Ed wouldn't have been surprised if they popped right out of his head and plunked on the table like two ceramic ball bearings.

"Holy fuck, you're like the Sunday crosswords with this shit. Fuck, I dunno. Why does the alcoholic leave the bar? More booze? *Free* booze?"

Ed smiled big and broad.

"You're smarter than you look."

"Better than looking smarter than I am, I suppose. But me no understand."

Ed just stared, knowing that it would come to the man.

And it did.

"Wait, you think that—what—one of these two is giving him girls? A fucking cannibal buffet?"

Ed shrugged.

"No think—I *know*. Why else would he leave his dungeon setup behind with no heat on him?"

Ed leaned forward and took another swig of his Rye.

"Was it the girl or the guy—Carson?"

"There's no way Mike would take orders or even instruction from this honey here. More apt to eat her, I'd say."

Ed leaned forward suddenly and jabbed a finger right between Carson's eyes.

"So this guy is our key."

Hugh leaned back, a smile on his face. He was obviously content, impressed with himself. But Ed didn't blame him. Truth be told, he was impressed by his partner as well. Puzzler or not, he hadn't expected Hugh to make the connections as quickly as he had, irrespective of the breadcrumbs Ed had dropped along the way.

Hugh suddenly became serious again.

"Okay, we've set up our organigram, sure. But we still don't know who the hell these people are, or how to find them. Which is what we *really* need to figure out."

"Oh, that's the easy part."

Hugh scoffed and rolled his eyes again.

"The easy part? Sure—sure it is. Colonel Mustard in—"

"No, really. Mac called me an hour ago. The fat guy in the Mickey Mouse shirt's name is Jonah Silvers."

Hugh scoffed.

"Give me a fucking break. You knew this all along?"

Ed chuckled.

"Sure did. And get this: last known place of employment? A crematorium, not more than two hours from here."

Hugh practically jumped to his feet.

"Well what the hell are we waiting for? Let's get going."

"Easy, Tonto. What are we gonna do? Run in there, guns a-blazin'? Let's get some rest tonight, head out tomorrow. I'll make a couple calls, see if I can get some help from the FBI."

"The FBI? Forget them, this is *our* case."

"Easy now, Hugh. Remember your first lesson of the day: we're detectives, we *detect*. Leave the rest to the grunts."

But despite his words, in the back of his mind, the idea of actually getting into some action appealed to Ed on some level.

Maybe...maybe we'll do more than detect this time.

PART II - Cloaks and Ghosts

Chapter 16

"NO...NOT ENOUGH. IT'S just not enough," Carson said, purveying the pile of bodies beside the oven. He counted twelve, not including the toddler.

Jonah had been right: his partner Vinny had come and gone without even questioning Carson's odd story about replacing Jonah in Scarsdale's basement. The thin, bird-like man hadn't even asked to see ID or bothered to inquire as to why Carson was piling the bodies instead of burning them.

Still, he knew that Vinny had about one or two more shipments before even someone as dull as he started asking questions. And Carson intended to deal with him before that happened.

If the man brought five or six more bodies, and adding Vinny himself to that number, then maybe—*maybe*—it would be enough. But then again, maybe it wouldn't. What Robert had managed to do back in the Harlop Estate—to somehow control the dead, not just with verbal orders, but to somehow go deep inside them, control them with his mind—well that was *something*.

And given their similar pedigree, Carson figured that he might be able to do the same. He just had to figure out how.

To his left, Michael breathed heavily, and Carson turned in time to see him wipe some filthy perspiration from his brow with the back of his hand. The man had a nasty bruise that ran from his temple to around his left eye from where the little bastard Allan had kicked him, and he looked like he hadn't slept in about a month.

"How many do we need? When is it going to be enough, Carson? Fifty? A hundred bodies? Will that be enough?"

Carson shrugged.

"The more, the merrier, as they say. Robert may have gotten the upper hand on us last time, but it won't happen again. We need to work fast, open the rift before Sean and the other Guardians block us."

"Block us?"

Carson shrugged.

"I wouldn't be surprised if Robert and his band of misfits are taking a more proactive approach. Just keep piling up the bodies, Michael." He bit his lower lip. He could tell that his little puppy was getting anxious, that Carson needed to throw him a bone to keep him satisfied soon. "Next time Vinny comes back with the bodies, help him move them down here. Then you can have him."

Michael raised an eyebrow, and even Bella moved away from him slightly.

"Have him?"

Carson chuckled.

"A snack, you know. Appetizer before the main course."

Michael smiled, and when he went back to stacking the corpses, he did it with a little more vigor.

***

"You remember when we first met, Bella?" Carson asked absently. He was lying beside her on the floor, their bodies drenched with sweat.

She turned to look at him. After the corpse had yanked out a large hunk of her hair, she had had no choice but to chop it all short. Despite her best efforts, and her uncanny dexterity with a blade, Bella had done a poor job of covering the bald area. And without her beautiful black hair, she had immediately been bumped down a grade on the attractiveness scale. Her severe eyebrows and the deep grooves around her mouth were more obvious, the scar on her temple more noticeable without the distraction of those shiny locks.

"Of course. You were a cocky juvie bastard, you know that?"

Carson smiled. He remembered the time well.

After murdering his foster parents, the state had done their best to try him as an adult, but leave it to the system to fuck that one up. He had confessed to stabbing his stepfather, who'd moonlighted as his stepmother's pimp and dealer, in the chest. When his stepmother had found him, he had slit her throat without a moment's hesitation. And yet he had only been sentenced to a psychiatric juvenile facility from the age of eleven to the age of maturity.

It was a joke, really. Everyone and their mother knew that Carson would kill again, the same way that he knew Robert would do the same after getting a taste of murder back at Seaforth.

Despite what Robert thought, or what the man struggled to convince himself of, they were cut from the same cloth, of the same genetic makeup.

Carson reached over and moved a thicket of Bella's hair over the bald area, which was still red and glistening.

Back in juvie, she had been straight, perfect. Back then, a young Dr. George Mansfield, loud and obnoxious, had been so negligent as to allow naive Bella, in just her first year of her psychiatry internship, to spend time with Carson alone.

Back then, Carson had only started to realize his potential, to understand his role to play in this world and the other. And so, evidently, had Bella.

"Remember when you taught me to meditate? To completely enter my own head?"

Bella nodded. As she did, the hair he had brushed over the bald spot fell away, and she quickly pushed it back.

"Can you help me go deeper, Bella?"

Bella appeared to contemplate this for a moment, her tongue pushing into her cheek.

"Maybe," she admitted at last. "Are you going to talk to your father again?"

Carson shook his head.

"I want to go there, Bella; this time, I want to enter the Marrow."

Bella sat bolt upright.

"You can't. You—"

Carson laughed.

"Look at you! So sensitive all of a sudden...are you worried about me? Worried that I won't come back? *Ha!* I only want to go there with my *mind*. I want to go *and* I want to come back, Bella. I *need* to come back—Leland can't open the rift from the Marrow. He needs us to help him."

"And we need Robert."

Carson nodded.

"That's right; we need a Guardian." He looked off to one side, thinking about what Leland had told him last time they had spoken, back when he had been locked up in Seaforth.

There were other Guardians out there, including that bastard Sean, but Robert was the most logical choice. Perhaps the only choice. "We need to find him, before he finds us."

Bella stared at him with her vibrant green eyes for what felt like an eternity.

"Yes," she finally said. "I can help you go deeper. But I have to warn you, the deeper you go, the greater risk of losing yourself."

Carson laughed again.

"Oh, my dear Bella, that's exactly why I *have* to go to the Marrow—to make sure that doesn't happen to me, to you, to anyone else."

Chapter 17

SOMETHING WASN'T SITTING WELL with Sean Sommers. It wasn't just the strange conversation with Aiden, although that was definitely part of it, but it was also something that the man in the cloak had said—or, as he called him, *the Cloak*. The man's words had sounded strange, just a little off, but he had been so transfixed by the book that at the time he hadn't thought anything of it.

But now it nagged at him, tugged at the corners of his mind. Wouldn't let him go.

Sean slipped a cigarette from the pack and brought it to his lips. He lit it, and then stepped out from under the streetlight and into the darkness that the side of the building offered. Puffing away, he turned his thoughts to the events of the past week or so.

For more than six decades, he had been a Guardian, imbued with the responsibility of keeping the status quo, of keeping the Marrow a one-way street. And for most of that time, his work had been uneventful. Like a well-worn pipe, there were occasional leaks, but Sean had managed to stem all of these before they became a flood. But ever since Leland had turned, things had gotten progressively worse. The man in the cloak was right; Robert should never have been brought in to deal with any of this. It was just too dangerous to get him involved. The prophecy decreed that a Guardian was needed to open the rift, and with their numbers dwindling to a new low, finding one was becoming a more and more difficult proposition for even someone as powerful as Leland.

There was Sean himself, but would never let himself be used as a vessel. He may have been old like Father Callahan, but he wasn't weak like the man had been. He was strong; Sean had seen much, and had lived through even more that scraped just below the threshold of detection by the human eye.

No, he would never let Carson or anyone before or after him use his body or quiddity to open the rift.

Robert, on the other hand...

He still wasn't entirely sure why he had gone to the man in the first place. He had told the Cloak that he had had no choice, that there were just too many quiddity for him to deal with on his own.

But that was only partly true.

There were more quiddity, certainly, but Robert hadn't been his only option. But like the words that the Cloak had said while reading the prophecy, something wasn't quite right and had nagged at him, at his mind, his thoughts, something that he hadn't been able to fully comprehend.

Something that had convinced him that it was Robert that he needed to recruit, despite the obvious risks. Despite knowing that Carson was locked away, and that Sean had rarely seen an apple fall hundreds of miles from the tree.

Sean took another drag, feeling the hot air swirl in his lungs. The cigarette almost done, he took another one out and used the end of the first to light it.

His mind turned next to what had gone wrong at Seaforth. From what he could gather, it was Peter the IT guy, the one that Sean and the man in the cloak, as the most influential Seaforth board members, had personally recommended, who had cracked. Who Carson and/or Leland had gotten to.

But all of this could have been moot if the Cloak had just let him kill Carson when he'd had the chance. But Sean's requests, as rational and clearheaded as they were, had gone unratified.

That is, until his encounter with Carson at Seaforth...but what other choice had he had? Locked away, Carson could only do so much. But loose? There was no way he could've let that happen. Even the Cloak realized this, as in spite of his proclivities for the Black brothers, his reaction to the man's death had been unexpectedly subdued.

And Sean had left nothing to chance. He'd believed that Robert would kill Carson in his cell, or else he would have never left them alone together. Part of him had hoped that they would have killed each other—two birds with one stone and all that—but Sean had never been that lucky.

Instead, he had ordered Aiden to blow up the prison as a safeguard measure, and Aiden hadn't hesitated.

Which brought him full circle.

It wasn't like Aiden to be obtuse on the phone; the man was as straightforward as they came. He followed his orders without questioning.

Something isn't right...

A car pulled into the lot of the building complex, and Sean flicked the cigarette behind him and slipped completely into the shadows. The vehicle was a dark blue sedan, one that he recognized from somewhere, but couldn't immediately place. Sean squinted hard. He could make out the outline of a driver and someone in the passenger seat, but he—

"Sean," a voice said from his left, and Sean whipped around, his hand going to the gun on his hip. He relaxed when he saw it was only Aiden standing a dozen feet from him. The man's hands were at his sides, and his expression, as usual, was deadpan. Like Sean, Aiden was standing in the shadows, and he failed to make out many of his features. His posture, his head shape, and his demeanor confirmed that it was him, however.

"Aiden," Sean replied curtly. "What happened at the Estate?"

Aiden hesitated, and Sean squinted harder. It wasn't like the man to be unsure of things, especially not when it came to answering Sean's direct questions.

There is something different about him.

"There was an...incident."

"Incident? What kind of incident?"

"An attack. Someone attacked the Estate. But I took care of them."

Sean couldn't believe what he was hearing.

"What? Who? What are you talking about, Aiden? Someone attacked Robert? Why the hell didn't you tell me this before?"

He took a step forward and Aiden bowed his head.

"It was Carson—he's back, and he wants Robert."

Sean's jaw dropped. If anyone else had uttered those words, he would have known it to be a lie, or worse, a terrible joke.

But not Aiden.

Aiden didn't lie, and Aiden definitely didn't joke.

"How...how is that possible? I thought..."

His mind flashed to the explosion at Seaforth, of the flames illuminating the storm clouds, reflecting off the heavy downpour.

It can't be.

When Sean spoke again, his voice was barely above a whisper.

"What the fuck happened, Aiden? What the—?"

Then Aiden stepped into the light and Sean almost fell backward.

"Fuuuuuck..."

The man's outline wasn't fully solid, and the light around him was wavering slightly.

Sean outstretched a finger and aimed it accusingly at the man.

"You're...you're..."

"Dead," Aiden finished for him.

Something slipped over his head from behind, a thick, coarse fabric, blinding him. Sean tried to turn, but before he could even move, something was driven into his spine—a fist, perhaps, or a foot—and he dropped to his knees. A rope was wrapped around his throat next, pinching the hood tight, while at the same time cutting off his air supply.

His hand went for his gun, but he found the holster.

"That's right, Sean," a familiar voice whispered in his ear through the thick fabric. "Aiden's dead, and you will be too if you don't do exactly what I say."

Sean wheezed, trying, but failing, to draw a full breath.

"Robert?" he gasped.

Chapter 18

"How many do you have this time?" Michael asked. The man before him was tall and thin, with a beak-like nose and beady eyes.

To Michael, he looked like an oversized rat.

"Eight. Eight more."

"Eight?"

The man nodded and moved to the back of the truck. It was a plain vehicle, not like the hearses seen in the movies. That was for the trip to the church, for appearances. After showing in the coffin, the bodies were removed, the pine boxes either sold or recycled, and the bodies were shipped here, to the crematorium, in a plain white cube van.

Or so Ratman had told him.

Michael's stomach growled as he waited for Vinny to unlock the back of the truck. It felt like a hundred years since he had bitten off Robert's index finger, and eons before that when he had nibbled on the girl in the cage.

His next meal was a long time coming, but now he was standing before him. Male meat wasn't his favorite—testosterone did something to sour the taste—but it would definitely tide him over.

Eight more bodies. Carson is going to be happy with number—he has to be.

Thinking of Carson brought Michael back to their first encounter outside his office building, and their subsequent discussions in the park and then in his car. His initial impression of the man as a deluded psychopath had been dispelled nearly the moment Carson opened his mouth. The man had a way of speaking, of drawing Michael in, and it didn't hurt that what he said was true; Michael *did* see something in the faces of his victims as their last breaths puffed out of them. And that air, that stale, often foul-smelling air expelled from their lipless mouths, was a sort of ether to him that rivaled the taste of their flesh on his tongue.

It was a noxious, addictive ether that he believed Carson could acquire for him in spades.

And this was all before he had actually seen the dead come to life, witness a woman with a whiskey bottle sticking out of her head stumble around as Bella flayed her with one of her many tiny knives.

If what Carson had said about the Marrow was true, then it was in his best interest to help the man in any way that he could. And if it meant that he got a little—just a wee little—snack along the way, then that was okay, too.

The smile on his face started to grow, despite the fact that it made the swollen skin on the side of his face and around his eye hurt.

"Hurry up, Vinny. Get the truck open and let's start chucking the bodies downstairs." Michael rubbed his sweaty palms on his pants as he waited impatiently for the man to act. He wasn't at all sure why this man Vinny, who, by all accounts, was one of the *others*, went along with what Carson said, but he didn't much care. If he put any thought to it, he might have come to the conclusion that it was Carson's strange charm, or his unwavering belief in a story, a mythos the likes of which Michael had never heard.

Vinny reached for the keys on his belt to unlock the back of the truck, but he dropped them onto the muddy ground.

His hands were shaking.

"Give me the fucking keys," Michael grumbled, shoving Vinny out of the way. It had only been a light push, but the man was off balance and slipped onto his ass.

He cried out, and Michael turned to face him.

"Get up," he instructed. A sound from the back of the truck drew his attention to the plain white door.

His eyes narrowed as he listened closely.

"Okay, okay! I'm getting up," Vinny replied quickly, but Michael hushed him and focused on the back of the truck.

Are the quiddity here already?

Carson had warned them that they would be coming faster now, especially after what Robert had done to the woman's body, commandeering her corpse. But Michael wasn't so sure.

Either way, there were no further sounds from the back of the truck, which he wasn't sure how to interpret.

He had definitely heard a dull thud only moments ago.

"What are you—?"

"*Shhh.*"

As he waited, he reached down for the keys on the ground and picked them up. He gave them a little jangle, and waited a little longer.

The only sound he heard was his stomach growling.

"Get over here," he said to Vinny. The man was pale, his rat nose twitching madly. "C'mon, get the fuck over here."

He tossed the keys at Vinny and they struck him in the chest. To both of their surprise, he managed to catch them.

Michael indicated the door with a flick of his wrist.

"Open it."

The man blinked rapidly and stepped in front of Michael, who receded several paces away from the truck.

Just in case, just in case.

In case of what, he didn't know.

Robert, maybe? Or whoever blew Jonah away?

When Vinny removed the lock and gripped the bottom of the door, ready to throw it up, Michael tensed, preparing himself for the worst.

Nothing happened. Vinny threw the door open and then he jumped back, as if he had also been expecting something to happen. Still nothing.

"Fucking rat," Michael grumbled, finally convinced that it must have just been the engine dying down, or a piece of mud dislodging from the wheel well. "Vinny, grab the first body, bring it downstairs."

Vinny pulled himself into the truck and then reached down and grabbed the first body. Three times the man had come with bodies since Michael had been at Scarsdale, and all three times the bodies had been in the thick black body bags. This time, however, the first body Vinny grabbed wasn't wrapped in anything at all. It was just a skinny blond guy with gray skin lain haphazardly on his back, his lifeless eyes staring at the ceiling of the truck. Vinny flipped the body up onto his shoulder, the corpse's head flipping unnaturally backward.

Fresh—very fresh.

"Hey, where are the bags?" Michael demanded as Vinny grunted and stepped by him.

"Cost-cutting measures," he said simply. He took one lurching step toward the door, then another.

Michael shook his head.

Reusing and selling caskets was something he could wrap his mind around, but skimping on body bags?

Fucking savages.

More hunger pangs struck him then, and he shook the thoughts from his head. The sooner they got the bodies out of the truck, the sooner he could have his "snack."

Michael moved toward the truck and pulled himself inside.

The smell was better than he had expected. It didn't smell great—much like a public restroom, it smelled heavily of chemicals that were barely doing an adequate job of covering up the scent of feces—but it wasn't horrible, either.

Michael quickly looked down at the bodies in the truck. There were nine of them, including two that couldn't have been older than ten years of age. As Vinny had said, none of them were in bags; they were just lying on the dirty plywood floor. Some had clearly rolled during the drive from wherever the hell Vinny had come—a funeral home, perhaps, or a cemetery—and one was sandwiched up against the inside wall, compressed there by the body of a naked and much fatter corpse.

Vinny can carry that one, Michael thought.

He reached for one of the younger corpses, a man who looked to be in his mid-twenties, and gripped him by the ankle. He was about to drag him toward the edge of the truck and hop out, to pull him onto his shoulder as Vinny had done moments ago, when he suddenly stopped short.

Eight. Eight more.

Michael's eyes whipped up. There were nine bodies in the truck, including the one that Vinny had carried away, that made ten.

And then one of the bodies sat up, and Michael stumbled backward. He fell out of the back of the truck, landing hard with an audible *schlop* in the muddy ground. He scrabbled to get to his feet, to extricate himself from the mud, when a figure appeared at the back of the truck.

He was holding a pistol in one hand and a gold shield in the other.

"Oh, hi there, Michael. We've been looking for you."

Chapter 19

"**WHAT THE FUCK IS** going on? Aiden, you brought them *here*? To this place? And you died? *What the fuck is happening?*"

Sean growled and moved his wrists up and down against the rope that bound them. The hood was actually some sort of thick bag, and it was stiflingly hot inside. Sweat dripped down his face and started to soak the material around his neck, which was still tightly tied by a second rope.

When he yelled, the sound was incredibly loud in his ears.

"How can you bring Robert here? He's been touched by Leland, you idiot! He can track him now. And if he finds—if he—"

"If he finds who?" demanded another voice that Sean recognized as Cal's.

"You! Cal, I should have fucking let you rot in Seaforth."

Something struck him on the crown of his head and stars spread across the sea of darkness that was his vision. Breathing heavily, he grunted and tried to keep his mind clear, despite the blow.

What the hell do they think they're doing? How...what...Carson's alive?

He swallowed hard, thinking back to what he had told the Cloak.

Carson's dead. Yes, I did it myself.

"Fuck," he swore, deciding to change tactics. "What do you want from me, Robert? Where are you taking me?"

This time, there was no answer.

Sean closed his eyes and tried to remain calm.

Only he couldn't do it. The anger that built up inside him was too great.

How could I be so stupid? Duped by Robert and his delinquent friends? By Aiden?

Sean thrashed against his bindings, and then threw his body forward. Completely blind, his face smashed up against what could have only been the back of the front seat. But this didn't stop him.

He had to get them to stop the car, to pull the hood off. To speak to him.

He immediately rocked to his left, jamming his shoulder up against the door. Something creaked, and he felt the window bow. Encouraged, he threw his body against the window again, and it bowed even more.

"He's going to break the fucking window! Grab him!"

Sean felt hands grab his arms, but he violently shook his shoulders back and forth, preventing them from getting a solid grip. He launched his head around blindly like a weapon, leading with his forehead, and eventually it cracked against something hard.

Someone cried out, and he felt something hot and wet soak the top of the bag. For a brief moment, the hands on his wrists released, and Sean took this opportunity to throw himself at the window for a third time.

It was an act of simple, blind rage. No forethought went into it, into the consequences; his only goal was for them to stop the car, to stop moving farther and farther away from likely the only person that could help them. The man who could protect them against Carson.

The Cloak.

The window shattered, and the hood was peppered with tiny cubes that bounced off of it like hail. The sound of the wind was suddenly deafening, and Sean rocked back to his original position. Dazed, he tried to move again, but before he could manage, something crashed down on the top of his head.

Only this time, it was hard enough to make an audible crack.

The last thought that passed through Sean's mind before he lost consciousness was that he hoped Aiden didn't touch him. That he wasn't well on his way to the Marrow to meet the man he had sent there more than three decades ago.

***

Lights. Halos. Stinging sweat in his eyes.

Sean blinked and rolled his head to one side, sending a splinter of pain from the crown of his head down to his ankles. He groaned, long and low, and then blacked out again.

***

Sean kept his eyes closed this time, and clucked his tongue. His mouth was so dry that he couldn't swallow. He tried to lick his lips, but his tongue was like Velcro.

"Water," he croaked. "Water."

A hand grabbed his chin and tilted it backward, sending a dull throb spiraling inside his skull. Water poured into his mouth, but it was so unexpected that he gagged and tried to tilt his head forward and spit it out. The hand on his chin, however, held firm and he gagged some more.

Eventually he was given a break to breathe, and he swallowed. More water came, a more reasonable amount now, and he gulped it down greedily.

With a sigh, Sean finally opened his eyes, blinking against the harsh light while at the same trying to survey his surroundings.

To plan an escape.

He was in some sort of gray room made of cement walls, maybe, or brick, with a single lone bulb hanging from the center of the room. His right shoulder ached from where he had smashed it against the door and window, and when he tried to move his arms, he realized that they were bound behind him now, and looped through the back of a metal chair.

They weren't taking any chances this time.

Aiden was standing by the door, leaning against the wall. When their eyes met, he spat a thin gray stream of tobacco juice onto the floor.

A dizzy spell hit him then, and Sean shut his eyes.

"We need to find Carson," Robert demanded. Sean slowly opened his eyes again and stared at the man, marveling at how different he was now compared to when they had met all those months ago.

Back then, Robert had been meek, obedient, shy and tentative. He had been untrusting, and reluctant to take the letter, let alone move into the Estate. It had been all about Amy back then, even though Sean had known that the girl was dead even before she pissed herself. What he didn't know, however, was how important a role the dead nine-year-old would play in the events to come.

But now, Robert had hardened, inside and out. His face was bruised, and the top of his ear was crusted with blood. One of his feet was pointed oddly to one side and his right hand was covered in gauze that had turned a deep brown.

Back then it might have been about Amy, but not anymore. Despite what he might say, it was about *him* now.

It was about Robert, and only Robert.

A chill suddenly traveled up and down Sean's spine as Robert Watts stepped forward and moved to within inches of his face.

"We need to find Carson, and you're going to fucking help us."

Chapter 20

CARSON'S BREATHING WAS SLOW, rhythmic, and this was what he focused on first. He imagined his lungs inflating, the air filling him like some sort of organic balloon, before being ushered back out again. As usual, thoughts started to enter his head: memories mixed with fantasy, of killing his stepfather, of his first kill in the woods that day with Buddy. In his mind, the people he killed were real monsters, the green, scaly kind with massive necks and throats, capable of devouring people whole.

"If a thought appears," Bella said in a monotone voice, "don't fight it. Instead, focus on it. Try to find where it is in your brain. Try to capture it with only your mind."

Carson did just that, and he found that chasing thoughts around in his neurons caused them to vanish.

They weren't real, after all; thoughts weren't real, tangible things. They appeared out of nothing, and disappeared into the void.

He took another deep breath. Then another. With every successive breath, a deeper, more complete darkness started to close in on him and the scattered thoughts became less and less frequent.

"Breathe deeper, Carson. Deeper...let the air fill not just your lungs, but your entire being."

Carson inhaled through his nose until it felt like his chest was the circumference of the Earth.

"Just when you think your lungs are full, inhale some more."

He was beginning to feel lightheaded and his entire body seemed to be hyper-oxygenated; his fingers were tingling, his toes numb.

"And deeper," Bella whispered in his ear.

His mind began to separate from his body, to become dis-embodied, as if he had injected a massive dose of ketamine and was slipping into the K-hole.

Only this was different.

Carson was still present, but not like he had been before; only his essence remained, his quiddity. Everything else had melted away.

His id, ego, and super-ego were all wrapped into one tight package, folded upon itself like DNA in a nucleosome.

Deeper he went, no longer hearing Bella, or feeling his own body.

A period of time elapsed, but he had no concept of how long. It could have been a minute, an hour, a day.

And then even a basic, rudimentary understanding of time disappeared.

Only Carson Black's id remained.

And then out of nothing came the Sea.

***

The sand was soft and warm on his feet.

"Leland? You here?"

It was so peaceful that Carson didn't want to move, let alone walk. The only thing he wanted to do was to stand and bask in the sun.

"Leland?"

He blinked slowly, and each time his lids separated, instead of becoming clear, his vision blurred, as if he were lowering his head into the water.

On the fifth or sixth such blink, the blurriness vanished, and Carson focused on a man in a black hat. Shadows covered his face, and his worn jean jacket was covered in a thin layer of sand.

"Carson...it's great to see you, my son."

And then he started to laugh, a grating sound that even made Carson cringe.

"Father, I need your help again."

The sky suddenly erupted into flames, and the soft, casual glow of the sun became a nearly unbearable inferno.

Sweat immediately broke out on Carson's brow.

Carson bowed his head, but the roaring flames drew Carson's eyes upward. In the roiling fire, he saw James Harlop's face, Andrew Shaw's, and finally, Jonah's.

The sight of the last man made his blood boil nearly as hot as the sky above.

"Robert's strong, too strong...he took control of one of the dead."

At the mention of his other son's name, Leland's head tilted upward slightly. Beneath the brim, Carson caught sight of his chin, but it wasn't scarred and sunburnt as he had imagined it might be. Instead, it was soft and smooth. When the head tilted a little more, he caught sight of a plump lower lip, red and full.

What the hell?

But then Leland lowered his head again, and the fleeting image was gone.

"Robert took control?"

"Yes. I need you to...to teach me how to do the same."

There was a pause, and Carson wiped sweat from his brow. He tried to move his feet, but they were glued to the tarry ground. He didn't panic. In fact, a small smile crossed his face. This was where he belonged, and where he would return one day with Leland in body and soul.

To rule like the prophecy foreshadowed.

"Carson, I can teach you, but what Robert did…it's not without risks, consequences. If you go too far…"

Carson raised an eyebrow toward his father's apprehension; this trepidation wasn't like him. On the few previous occasions he had gone deep enough to transport his mind to the Marrow, the man had been unrelenting in his need to generate a rift. His desire had been all-encompassing.

Carson's eyes drifted upward and he stared at the faces molded in fire.

Everyone else before me has failed.

"I won't let you down, Father. I will open the rift."

Leland didn't reply right away, leaving Carson to listen to the roaring fire above and the churning sea behind him.

"The longer you stay here, the more likely they are to *feel* it," Leland said at last. "And the longer we wait to open the rift, the more likely it is that *he* will foil our plans."

Carson nodded; there was no need to clarify who the 'he' his father spoke of was.

Sean Sommers.

Leland's black hat lowered, and when he spoke again, his voice had dropped several octaves.

"Leave Sean to me."

Carson swallowed hard and nodded.

"Where is Robert now?"

"He's…he has left the Harlop Estate, heading east. But there is something else…*someone* else with him, *in* him. Blocking me. I can't…I can't pinpoint him."

Leland extended his right hand, and for a split second what Carson saw was no longer a human hand. In its place was dark and leathery, extending in three long, pointed talons.

"Someone is blocking me," Leland repeated, and he made a fist, his hand returning to its typical human form.

Carson's mind flicked to the scene of the woman grabbing the fucking kid with the glasses back at the Harlop Estate, and the way she had been drawn to Robert shortly before Carson had lost control of her.

And Robert had taken over.

He gritted his teeth. It was that woman's quiddity that was blocking Leland, he was sure of it.

Somehow Robert had implanted her in his head.

"I won't fail you, Father. Now tell me how to control the dead...tell me how I can free you and all of our brothers and sisters from this place."

Chapter 21

"YOU GUYS THINK YOU know something? You think you know what's at stake here?" Sean hissed. "You don't know anything. I should have killed you when I had the chance. If I'd known that you would get this fucked up, Robert, that you would go looking for the very man that wants to use you to destroy the world, I would have shot you dead on your doorstep that first time we met."

Robert had his back turned when he spoke to him, but mentioning that first encounter must have struck a chord with him, because he whipped around. In a second, he was on Sean, his hands digging in deep into his thighs as he leaned in close.

"Well you didn't, did you?"

Sean tried to look away, but Robert grabbed his face, pinching his cheeks hard. He stared him directly in the eyes.

"Didn't you?"

"No," Sean managed, and then shook his face away.

"No, no you didn't. Now you're going to help us find Carson, or Aiden here is going to give you a nice, big fat hug. How 'bout that?"

Sean glanced to Aiden, but the man didn't react outside of providing what was quickly becoming his patented response: spitting on the floor. Sean took a deep breath.

"He can't be here, Robert. You know this. The longer he stays, the—"

"I don't give a shit!" Robert suddenly screamed, and Sean recoiled.

The man had changed, that was for sure, but this was insane. It was a completely different person standing in front of him.

What the hell happened to him?

He had been pissed when they had all left Seaforth, but he hadn't been like *this*.

What the fuck happened to him?

Cal, who had been watching off to one side with his arms crossed over his chest up to this point, suddenly stepped forward and reached for Robert's arm.

Robert shrugged him off.

"Where's Carson, Sean? Are you going to tell me where the fuck he is?"

Sean shrugged as best he could given his restraints.

"How the fuck should I know? I thought he was fucking dead! *You* said he was dead! You said you shot him in Seaforth, remember? Goddammit, Robert, I fucking wish we had left you on that island. Every minute—every *second* that you're still alive is a second closer Leland is to opening the rift."

"Yeah, maybe you shouldn't have fucking killed him, then, did you ever think about that?"

Sean grimaced.

"You think you know what happened? You think you know *anything*? Let me tell you something, you fucking punk, if it weren't for the Cloak, then—" Sean clamped his mouth shut. He had started to ramble; he had let this man, this *nobody*, get under his skin. And he had said too much.

Perhaps Robert wasn't the only one who had changed.

Robert had started to walk away when Sean began his diatribe, but now he turned back.

"The Cloak? You mean the man in the hat? You mean Leland?"

Sean remained tight-lipped.

"Who are you talking about, Sean?"

Robert threw his arms up.

"Aiden, any ideas on how to get this man to talk?"

Like Sean, Aiden said nothing.

"Sean, things have changed. We need to get to Carson before he comes for us. Do you understand that? We can't just sit around anymore while he collects more of his freaks, wrangles more of the dead. In fact, if it weren't for Aiden over there, we'd be dead already," Cal said, his voice surprisingly calm.

"Yeah, and who do you think told him to watch out for you, huh? Yeah, that's what I thought."

Something crossed over Robert's face, and when he spoke next, he had regained some semblance of control.

"If you won't find Carson, then tell me where the book is."

Sean pressed his lips together even tighter, as if allowing them to open would somehow make him more tempted to actually speak. Robert's fists clenched and unclenched, and Sean knew that the man was on the verge of lashing out physically.

That was fine by him. It wouldn't be the first time he was beaten, and it had been done by bigger and badder men than this fucking accountant standing before him.

But instead of punching him, Robert turned and walked to the door. He passed Aiden without saying a single word, then left the room.

It clanged closed behind him, and then the three of them were left in silence. For a long while, no one said anything, but as Sean had predicted, Cal couldn't keep his mouth shut forever.

"Fuck, Sean, just help us find Carson. Trust me, we know the stakes. Please."

Sean eyed the man.

"Why the change of heart all of a sudden? Two weeks ago, you guys wanted to put this shit behind you. Now what? Got an itch?"

Cal sighed and rolled his shoulders.

"For the record, I was always in. But now…things are different, ever since Shelly—"

And then it was Cal's turn to clam up.

It was only then that Sean realized that the kid in the glasses and Shelly were missing from this whole scene.

This whole gang of ghostbusting delinquents.

"What? They gave up? Shelly and the boy?"

Cal's face hardened.

"No. The boy is gone. Fucking asshole Carson sicked the dead on him, sent him to the Marrow."

Sean said nothing. The boy had known the risks; he himself had explained them to him before transporting Allan to Seaforth.

Still, another dead meant another notch in Leland's belt, another potential soldier for him to use in the great war that was to come.

As for Shelly…

"What happened to Shelly?"

Cal looked away, and in that instant Sean knew that something *had* happened to her. She hadn't been sent to the Marrow, that much was certain, but something else had happened. Something that had sent Robert into a tailspin. Sean racked his brain, recalling how the two had interacted when he was in their presence. They had been close, *were* close; he knew as much based on how Robert had protected Shelly both in the helicopter and at Seaforth.

Had she left him? Was that it?

He posed the question to Cal, who suddenly became angry, similar to how Robert had acted only moments ago.

"Tell us where he is, Sean! Tell us where the fuck Carson is hiding out! We know that you can reach out to him. *Now just tell us where he is!*"

Sean observed the man carefully. Cal's hands were twitching at his sides, but not aggressively, like Robert's had. This was different.

Frustration, maybe? Or jealousy? Why is Robert so mad? He was only this upset when he found out about Amy, when—

Sean sat bolt upright and pulled hard against his restraints.

"She's pregnant, isn't she? For fuck's sake, tell me Shelly isn't pregnant!" The ropes dug in deep to his wrists, but this only made him pull harder. "Tell me he wasn't that stupid!"

When Cal looked away briefly, Sean knew that his words rang true.

And then another revelation came to him, the thing that had bothered him about what the Cloak had said, when he had read the prophecy.

Only the quiddity of a child, of a powerful child born of two Guardians, will be able to hold it open and allow souls to pass into the world of the living.

Two Guardians.

Two fucking Guardians, not one.

Sean's vision suddenly went red.

It wasn't Amy that Leland intended to use to hold the rift open, but this unborn child. Shelly and Robert's child, the child of *two* Guardians.

"Where's Shelly now?" he asked, his heart racing so hard in his chest that he could barely get the words out.

Cal froze, but didn't turn.

Sean pulled against the ropes so hard that the wooden chair creaked. Then he jumped forward, all four chair legs coming a full inch off the ground. Aiden finally took notice and stepped away from the wall.

"Shelly! Where is Shelly?!" he yelled. He hopped again, and this time he felt the legs beneath him flex a little. "Robert! *Robert*! Get the fuck back in here! *Where is Shelly?!*"

Chapter 22

WARDEN BEN TRISTAN WASN'T sure where he was. In fact, he wasn't at all sure what had happened to him. The last thing he remembered was the horrible scene of his friend, of Father Callahan, being torn apart, and Carson Ford performing some sort of black, voodoo magic to keep him alive.

And then the square-headed bastard pushed him into the void, and he had awoken on a beach, of all places.

Am I dead? Is this heaven?

It certainly felt like heaven. It had been a long time since he had been to a beach—a beach outside of the rocky shores of Seaforth Prison, that is. Having spent most of the last decade squirreled away inside the gray cement walls of the prison, Ben was as pale as they came and he didn't do well in the heat. But the weather here, wherever he was, was simply perfect: warm and sunny, without being overbearingly hot.

And the sand was like velvet pearls beneath his feet and between his toes. He looked down then, and was surprised to see that he was barefoot. He was still wearing his warden uniform, which was strangely not uncomfortable even though it was designed for a much cooler climate. His pants were rolled up to the bottom of his calf—his calves were too thick for them to be rolled any higher—but he couldn't remember doing that.

Ben turned his head to the surf next, his smile slowly transitioning into a frown. Even if he had forgotten everything that had happened before arriving on the beach, even if he remembered driving to the beach, looking at that surf, he would have known that something wasn't quite right.

It was the waves; the water broke exactly the same way on each and every wave. As he glanced along what appeared to be an infinite shoreline, Ben saw that, like some sort of bizarre optical illusion, the waves were always the same. *Exactly* the same.

Ben blinked hard, then rubbed his eyes with the heels of his hands.

I'm either dead or unconscious; in a coma, maybe.

He shrugged. Either way, there wasn't much he could do about it now.

"Hello? Hello?" His voice reflected across the identical whitecaps and bounced back at him. He cupped his mouth with his hands. *"Hello? Anyone out there?"*

Predictably, his call went unanswered.

Ben moved toward the water, testing it first with his big toe. It was incredibly warm and inviting, like bath water.

He put his entire foot in next, and before he knew it, he was up to his ankles.

A thought suddenly flashed in his mind.

Replenish the stock, give up yourself for the greater good.

Ben scrunched his face. It was such a weird thing to pop into his head at that moment, so foreign, that it made him stop his forward advance and look around.

The water rippled about his ankles, even though he was no longer moving, and the perpetual waves seemed to have calmed around him.

Ben shook his head and took another step forward. It seemed that the deeper he went, the less feeling he had in his legs, as if the warm water was like Novocaine for his skin.

At first it was pleasant, but as he continued to move, it became unnerving, a sensation that gave him pause.

What the hell am I doing here?

The water was close to his rolled-up pants now, and when he looked down to see if the hem had gotten wet, he noticed something in the water.

At first, Ben thought it was a fish, a bright green fish of some sort. Intrigued, he bent at the waist, trying to make out the details. It certainly shared the same shape as a fish; it was about six or eight inches long, with a large head and a thin tail. The tail itself was made up of bright yellow fins, with iridescent webbing between the individual spines. In his limited spare time, Ben had been an avid fisherman, although with his post at Seaforth, he hadn't been out in a long while. The last time he had been fishing had been in early February, when he and Quinn had drilled a hole in the ice and had a few beers. The only thing they had caught was a buzz and a chill.

Quinn...

Ben shook his head, not wanting to go down memory lane in this strange place. Instead, he focused on the fish, which, the longer he stared, seemed less and less like anything he had ever seen before. For one, it didn't at all appear intimidated by him; instead, it seemed energized by his presence, weaving in and out of the space between his legs. It was a broad fish, and from his vantage point, it looked to Ben to only be about the width of a slice of bread. It was hypnotic the way it fluttered through the water, vibrating along its length, but when it passed in front of him this time, it stopped moving and seemed to hover. A strange compulsion suddenly overcame Ben, and he went to grab for it.

But he never touched it. Instead, as soon as his fingers neared the surface of the water, something changed.

The fish suddenly flipped onto its side and its color transitioned to a whitish green. For a split second, Ben thought that it had died, that it had undergone the paling process that all dead fish did as they floated to the surface.

But then the side of the fish flickered, and a dozen eyes suddenly opened.

And they weren't fish eyes. They were human eyes. In fact, they looked very much like the blue eyes that Carson had held in his palms what seemed like a decade ago.

Quinn's eyes.

Ben retracted his hand and stood bolt upright, his heart racing, sweat instantly forming on his brow. The fish righted itself, and then with startling speed darted out of sight.

Swallowing hard, Ben tried to understand what he had just seen. But nothing he could think of helped him rationalize the experience. Suddenly feeling uncomfortable in the warm water, he started to backpedal toward the shore. He was almost on the sand again when he heard a voice from behind him and whipped around.

"Hi."

Ben squinted against the bright sun and exited the water completely.

A mirage?

The kid before him looked real enough, though, complete with Coke bottle spectacles. Thin, young, and pale despite the sun.

"Hi," he repeated, his expression neutral. "My name's Allan. Allan Knox."

Chapter 23

"**WAKE UP! CARSON,** *WAKE the fuck up!*"

The words filtered down to him as if through a long tunnel or a tin can.

"*Carson!*"

He felt his body rocking, as if he were surfing on the very waves that he and his father were so desperate to avoid.

I can teach you...but it's not without risks, consequences.

A smile appeared on Carson's lips, and he slowly opened his eyes. Bella was hovering over him, her face inches from his. Her fingers dug into the tops of his arms.

"Carson?" she said, repeating his name as a question this time. She released him and tried to pulled away, but Carson reached up and wrapped his arms around her waist. Then he kissed her full on the lips. She grunted, and then wrangled herself free.

"Carson, what the fuck are you doing? Get up!"

She scrambled to her feet, and Carson stood beside her. He was nude, and reached for his underwear that sat atop his pile of clothes. As he put them on, Bella started to ramble.

"Fucking hell, you won't believe what the fuck happened when you were out. The goddamn guy Vinny brought cops back with him! They're upstairs right now, and they've got Michael."

She was breathing heavily, on the verge of hyperventilating. He couldn't remember ever seeing her like this before.

"Calm down, Bella. Calm down—I can barely understand you. The cops? They're upstairs?"

Bella nodded, her eyes still wide.

"Michael's stalling them, but I can hear them talking right outside the door. They're gonna come inside, Carson. I don't know what the fuck Vinny said to them, but they're here—and they know that you're here, too. I don't know how, but they *know*."

Carson frowned. He wasn't fond of cops for obvious reasons.

"How many are there?"

"Two—two that I know of. But you know cops. Always calling in their friends. Could be more on their way."

This eased some of Carson's anxiety. The last time he had been taken in, it had required a baker's dozen boys in blue.

"Two men." He drew in a deep breath, then shook out his entire body. "Okay, Bella, let's go."

She screwed up her face.

"Go where? Did you not hear me? Did you lose your mind talking to the Goat?" She gestured about the soot-covered crematorium. "We're trapped down here. They're upstairs, just outside the door. Unless you know of a secret passage, we are *fucked*."

Carson eyed Bella.

"Have you no faith, Bella?"

"Faith? *Faith*?"

Carson ignored her incredulity. Then he strode toward the staircase.

"Carson? *Carson*? Fuck!" Bella shouted.

But as he made his way up the stairs, she followed close behind.

His smile returned.

***

"Keep those hands up," Carson heard someone say from directly outside the door. The glass was one-way, designed to keep prying eyes out of the crematorium. From his vantage point, Carson could only see Michael from the side, his hands high in the air as instructed. He couldn't see who had ordered him to stay put.

Carson turned to Bella.

"You sure that Vinny brought bodies back?"

Bella nodded.

"What are you going to do?"

"You'll see. Just stay behind me."

Before she had a chance to protest, Carson threw the door wide and stepped out into the muddy afternoon.

"Gentlemen," he proclaimed, his arms out wide, showing that he had no weapons. "What seems to be the problem here?"

"Freeze!"

Carson ignored the command, and continued walking until he was standing next to Michael, who was looking over at him, a strange expression on his face.

"Freeze or I will shoot!"

This time, Carson stopped and surveyed the scene.

Two men stood about ten feet away from him and Michael. They were typical cops, or maybe detectives. One of them was older, early fifties, maybe, wearing an ugly plaid blazer. The other was younger, handsome, and obviously green based on the way he was holding his pistol as if it owed him money. Clearly, they had been waiting for Carson to come out of the building, otherwise they would have taken him into custody by now.

"And now, the obligatory man in his underwear appears," the younger man said with a grimace. Carson heard the door open behind him, but didn't turn. He kept his eyes locked on the younger detective's.

"Ah, and of course, there *you* are. Brutal haircut, by the way. Why don't you go stand in line there beside your boyfriends?"

Bella did as she was instructed, her arms preemptively held high. Carson shot her a look, a reassuring smile, letting her know that everything was going as planned. She shook her head.

"And now we just need the pedo in the Mickey shirt and we'll be all set." The young man cast a glance toward the door that Bella and Carson had come out of moments ago. "He in there with you?"

"Who? Jonah? Yeah, he had a bit of an accident."

"Accident?"

Carson shrugged.

"Someone blew a hole in his chest."

Neither detective reacted to the comment.

"Let me ask you something, detectives—is that right? You *are* detectives, aren't you?"

They didn't answer, but the older man's expression relaxed for a split second.

"Ah, yes, detectives. Listen, you guys deal with a lot of death, right? I mean, you"—he indicated the younger man with his chin—"look like someone from New York or maybe Chicago? That about right? Yeah, I can see it in your face. So you must've seen a lot of death in your time. Have you—?"

"Enough small talk," the older man instructed. "Get on your knees and interlace your fingers behind your head."

"It's rude to interrupt," Carson told the man. But he did as he was ordered, his knees making a suctioning sound in the mud. In his periphery, he saw Bella and Michael do the same.

"I hope you have a fucking plan," Michael grumbled just loud enough for him to hear.

"When you're young, they tell you things, teach you about what they think is right, about life and death. They tell you—"

"Hey, Preacher Tom, shut the fuck up and put your hands behind your head, okay?"

Carson interlocked his fingers. He let his eyes wander between the two detectives, his focus now on the back of the cube truck, the door of which was still raised. Inside, he could see the outline of several bodies. There were heavy shadows, indistinct, but he counted at least six of them.

More than enough.

And for some reason they weren't even in body bags.

Even better.

"Growing up, they tell you that life is precious, unique, that you should savor every moment. They tell you that when you die it's a one-way street." As he spoke, he closed his eyes and began to breathe deeply, just as Leland had told him. The detective said something, but he focused inward, and didn't pick up the words. He reached out for the Marrow, remembering the brine in the air, the soft sound of the waves crashing.

"They tell you that once you get to the afterlife, you will be rewarded, you will be given your little fucking slice of Heaven. But what they *don't* tell you is that what you experience is actually Hell."

Carson's mind skipped along the waves, and he slowly started to draw up an image of the back of the truck, the outlines of the bodies. As his focus deepened, he began to make out forms on the beach; not six, but eight figures, all standing, heads low, not speaking, not moving.

Got you, he thought. *I got you all.*

"They lied," he continued. "Death isn't a one-way street."

With his mind, Carson locked on to the lost quiddity, and then he took in a giant breath and returned to his body.

Only he didn't come back alone.

"Jesus fuck!" he heard someone shout, followed by the sound of heavy footsteps on the truck bed. He opened his eyes just in time to see the younger detective spin around as one of the dead literally fell out of the truck. Awkward, like a newborn calf, it tried to rise, but collapsed again.

"What the fuck!" he screamed, falling backward as the rest of the dead in the truck pulled themselves to their feet.

He pinched off two shots, one of which struck the closest corpse with a dull thunk, while the other one pinged off something metal.

"Ed! Jesus fucking Christ, what the fuck!"

The other detective, the more seasoned one, had been diligent, controlled, keeping his sights on Michael the entire time his partner was screaming and firing. But he made a fatal error.

The man that the younger man had called Ed looked to witness the horrors shambling from the back of the truck. It was a subtle gesture; he didn't even turn his head all the way around. But it was still too far.

Bella sprang to her feet and then literally flew across the distance between them as graceful as a ballerina, only far deadlier.

She grabbed the man's front shoulder and spun him, while at the same time taking up residence behind him. The man twisted to one knee, and that was when she slipped the blade out and pressed it to the base of his throat.

The man dropped his gun.

"Greenhorn?" Carson said, rising. "I think you should follow your partner's lead and drop your gun, don't you?"

"So much for just fucking 'detecting,'" Carson heard the younger detective say before dropping his gun to the ground.

Chapter 24

"ROBERT, YOU HAVE TO let me go. Please, I need to go see the Cloak. There's been some sort of...mistake," Sean pleaded. His mind was working a mile a minute, trying to figure out and understand the implications of their error.

Robert had since rushed back into the room where Sean was held captive, if for no other reason than to get him to stop yelling. Only when he appeared, his face wasn't etched in fear as Sean had hoped it would be; instead, his eyebrows were lifted high on his forehead, his reaction one of surprise.

"Who the hell is the Cloak?" he demanded, to which Sean just shook his head.

"Please, I need to speak to him. I need to see the book again."

The mention of the book had clearly piqued his interest, but Sean decided to take a different approach.

"Look, you take me to see the Cloak, you let me read the book, and if after all that you still want to hunt down your brother, I'll help you."

Robert's eyes narrowed, and Sean wondered if he could see through his lies.

"So you know where he is."

Sean shook his head.

"I didn't say that. But I can...I am very good at finding people, Robert. You of all people should know that."

Robert seemed to mull this over, chewing his lip. But before he came to a decision, Cal sidled up to him and whispered something in his ear. Robert nodded to his friend.

"Well? Are you going to let me go?"

Robert glanced to Aiden next, who had resumed his post by the door. There was a silent exchange of sorts, of the like Sean was not privy.

"Who the hell is this 'Cloak'? Is it another one of your goons? Is this all a ploy to get one of your henchmen to come and take us out?"

Sean sighed.

"Robert, it—"

Robert stepped toward him again.

"A few minutes ago, you were yelling that you should have killed me"—he gestured to the others in the room—"that you should have just killed all of us. And now what? I'm supposed to believe that you've had a change of heart? What gives, Sean?"

Sean pressed his lips together defiantly, and Robert turned to Cal next.

"What'd you say to him?" he said, his words dripping with accusation. Cal averted his eyes and shrugged.

"Didn't say nothin', just..."

Cal's words faded as a sudden pressure in Sean's chest drew all of his attention. He squeezed his eyes tight, and the cement room in which he was held immediately fell away and a foreign scene flashed across his vision.

Two gunshots, a scream. A man with a 'Y' incision stumbling awkwardly, falling to the muddy ground.

A wide smile, Cheshire-like in proportions.

More shouts.

Sean's eyes snapped open and focused on Robert. The man was also grimacing, and it was obvious that he had felt something as well.

There had been another ripple in the Marrow, something that wasn't quite right. Only this one was more powerful than with the Harlops, or even at Seaforth.

Carson *was* alive; Sean was sure of it now. Only a Guardian could have caused such a stir.

"You feel that?" he gasped, knowing the answer before he even asked the question. Robert nodded, and the man cleared his throat, trying to play off the pain.

This surprised Sean; most of the other Guardians he had known over the years felt these ripples in the Marrow as a twinge, a palpitation, or just a feeling that something *wasn't right*. But Robert was different; like Sean, Robert felt it in his very *core*.

"He can't stay here," Sean said at last, clearly meaning Aiden. "Carson has done something, *is* doing something, and we don't have much time. The longer —"

"He stays, at least until you tell us what you want, until you tell us where Carson is."

Sean closed his eyes again and shook his head. Despite the revelation, he couldn't give Robert the information he so desperately sought. At least, not until speaking to the Cloak.

The Cloak would know what to do.

Sean resigned himself to lowering his head. It was clear that he wasn't going to get anywhere with these men, at least not with his current approach.

"Robert, the Cloak is a Guardian, just like you and me. Been around for even longer than me, if you can imagine. And I need to go speak to him."

Robert crossed his arms over his chest, but despite the gesture, Sean knew that he had captured the man's interest.

But Cal was the one who spoke up first.

"And why, pray tell, do you so desperately need to see this mysterious caped crusader all of a sudden?"

Sean didn't take his eyes of Robert when he answered.

"Because...because it's not Amy that Leland needs, but Shelly's baby."

Robert stopped pacing and he turned to face Sean.

"What are you talking about? He already has Amy, *my* daughter."

Sean sighed.

"Robert, you don't understand...the prophecy, the prophecy doesn't say *a child of a guardian will hold the rift open,* but *a child of Guardians. Guardians, plural.*"

Robert stopped his forward advance.

"What are you saying, Sean?"

"What I'm saying is that Shelly is a Guardian, Robert. And Leland doesn't need Amy, but he needs the unborn baby in Shelly's belly."

Chapter 25

THE DETECTIVE'S GUN LANDED in the mud with an audible splat.

"What the fuck is going on?" Hugh stammered. He tried to backpedal away from the truck, but his heel snagged and he fell on his ass. Then he froze and stared as the seven corpses flowed out of the back of the truck. Some landed awkwardly on their feet, while others simply fell face first, not even bothering to brace themselves for impact. Although they all took a unique, uncoordinated route from the truck bed to the ground, they had more in common than their horribly pale flesh, wounds, and smeared makeup from the funeral viewings: no matter how clumsily they fell, they eventually pulled themselves to their feet.

Even to Carson, these dead were a ghastly sight. There were five males and one female, and two whose gender was hard to make out based on the level of decomposition.

Jesus, did Vinny dig these ones up himself?

Detective Hugh had put a bullet in the chest of the only woman, but it hadn't even fazed her.

"Run, Hugh! Run!" the older cop shouted, but it was too late for little Hugh.

Michael slipped an arm around his waist and hoisted him to his feet. The detective didn't struggle, didn't even object to being manhandled. Carson caught a glimpse of both detectives' faces, both restrained, and marveled at how pale they had become.

"Well, this is not how you saw this going down, I reckon," Carson said with a laugh.

"Should we let them at 'em?" Bella asked, indicating the dead that had since risen to their feet.

It was a sight that Carson doubted he would ever become comfortable with, no matter how many times he witnessed it: the dead bodies standing there, their heads low, their hands dangling limply at their sides, occasionally twitching like someone with advanced Tourette's.

Waiting for instructions. For *his* instructions.

"No, don't think so, Bella. I think we should keep these guys alive for a little while longer. Might come in handy."

Michael's expression soured, and Carson remembered his promise to the man.

"I said you could have Vinny, not these men. Where is he?"

Michael shook his head, the frown a permanent fixture on his face now.

"Don't know. Bastard set us up and then left. I think he went inside, but can't be sure. You didn't see him?"

Carson shook his head. He and Bella had been downstairs, and there are plenty of places for even Ratman to hide on the ground level. He stepped forward and addressed the detectives—Vinny could wait.

"Tell me, gentlemen, are you here on your own, or are you expecting friends?"

Hugh looked pale on the verge of translucency, and had resorted to staring at the mud in front of him. The second detective, Ed, looked embarrassed at being overtaken by Bella.

Don't worry, fella, you aren't the first and won't be the last.

When there was no immediate answer, Carson walked over to the man in the hideous sportscoat that could now list mud speckles to its list of endearing attributes. As he approached, Bella's grip on his hair tightened and the blade tickled his Adam's apple. Carson squatted on his haunches so that he was at eye level. When he reached out, the man recoiled as best he could given Bella's grip.

Carson gently brushed some salt-and-pepper hair from the man's temple.

"You better answer me, detective. And you better tell the truth, because, trust me, I won't have to tell sweet Bella here twice to cut out your windpipe. So, what do you say? Have someone on the way? More cops, maybe? FBI?"

At the mention of the FBI, the man's eyes dropped from Carson's, which in his book was as good as a nod.

"Ah, okay. FBI. How many, then? One, two? Ten?"

The man didn't answer and Carson shook his head.

"This isn't charades, Detective. You best answer me, or I'll have Bella—wait, you know what?" He turned to Michael, who had Hugh in some sort of modified rear-naked choke. "Michael? I don't think our detective friends believe we are serious. Why don't you show them? Just a little taste?"

Michael didn't hesitate. He leaned forward and clamped his incisors down on Hugh's ear. The man howled and finally started to struggle, but Michael's grip held him firm. As he screamed, the dead started to twitch more frantically, but Carson kept them at bay with his thoughts.

Michael lifted his chin and Carson saw Hugh's ear start to stretch unnaturally. The man's screams intensified as his entire scalp started to lift, and out of the corner of his eye, Carson noticed that the other detective, immobilized by Bella's knife, lowered his head.

With one final tug, and one last howl from Hugh, the top third of the man's ear tore away. There was far less blood than Carson would have expected, but there was enough of it to turn his sideburns and temples red.

Carson had to give the man credit; to his surprise, he refrained from anything more than a whimper after the chunk was removed. When Michael started to chew loudly, his mouth partway open, Carson turned his attention back to Ed, and indicated for Bella to raise his head.

She obliged, a smile on her pretty face. When she was smiling, he could almost overlook the missing chunk of hair.

"Now do you believe that we're serious? Hmm? I bet you do. So tell me, fine sir, how many FBI officers should we be expecting?"

When the man replied, his voice was low, bordering on a whisper.

"Just one," he admitted. "Just one."

"Good. Now that wasn't so hard, was it?"

Chapter 26

SHELLY KNEW EVEN BEFORE the steam cleared from the shower that Robert was gone. She felt it in her gut. Unlike when the quiddity were near, this wasn't a tightness, *per se*, but more of a release, a strange calming sensation that overcame her.

And, ironically, it was unnerving.

The thin veneer of calm didn't last long.

"Goddammit!" she shouted, tossing her hairbrush at the mirror. It shattered, but the fragments remained glued in place. The loud noise gave her pause, and she took a moment to stare at her reflection, knowing that her reaction was, at least in part, driven by her hormonal changes.

Her breasts, full to begin with, had grown thicker, more full, and her nipples were dark and swollen. Her belly was not as large as she might have expected at nearly five months along, but she chalked this up to being full-figured to begin with.

With a heavy sigh, she regained control of herself. A part of her knew that Robert was right, that she shouldn't be out chasing ghosts in her present state.

It was just too risky.

But another part of her couldn't stand being alone, of not being part of the team anymore.

So what if I'm pregnant? I'm still important. I'm still a valuable member of the team. I still have a fucking brain, don't I?

Somewhere outside, she heard the gate at the bottom of the drive squeak open. With a deep breath, Shelly resisted the urge to run down there, shake a broomstick in the doorway like some crazed witch, and beg Robert and Cal and Aiden, who she knew had all gone with him like a fucking Boy Scout troop, to take her with them.

She knew Robert well enough.

He would simply drive off without her, leaving her embarrassed, ashamed, and alone, instead of just the latter.

Instead, she performed her post-shower routine, trying to regain some semblance of normalcy. She dried her body with the coarse towels that felt like they had been made of porcupine quills, then brushed her short blonde hair straight.

Getting dressed proved to be an adventure, as she had yet to shop for new clothes. She told herself that she hadn't had time, which given their activities of the last little while wasn't untrue, but deep down she knew a large part of it was because she was in denial.

After all, Shelly had never had any designs of becoming a mother. No, she was quite content in living her life as a free spirit, a transplanted hippie, if you will.

Of spending her hours banishing quiddity to the other side.

Her tumultuous relationship with her biological mother prior to the adoption process had soured the notion of motherhood long ago. And besides, who wanted to be beholden to an infant? A suckling babe that, if left alone for a day, maybe even less, would perish? A fucking amoeba, one that if you poked, it reacted, but otherwise it just shat itself and cried when it was hungry? Who could be expected to love *that*?

Being a mother was the most anti-feminist thing on Earth.

Yet her feelings for the child, for children in general, now that one had been implanted in her, had warmed slightly, and her rhetoric was used as more of a defense mechanism rather than a credo to live by. It wasn't love, not quite—love was something that was to be worked for, like a plant, groomed, blossomed, given space and time to grow—but it was *something*.

Something new, something strange, something oddly *good*, in a world shrouded in *bad*.

Shelly squeezed into her leather pants, threw a loose blouse on top, and was about to leave the room when she saw something on the bedside table, *her* bedside table, that hadn't been there before.

It was an old photograph, and the image, although black and white, had yellowed slightly around the edges.

As Shelly made her way toward it, she realized that her hands were starting to shake, even though she couldn't make out the details yet.

There was just something about the way it was propped up against the alarm clock, the way it had been folded and was now creased…

When Shelly picked it up, she started to cry.

It was her, of course, and everything suddenly made sense: the pressure she felt when the quiddity were around, the way she had intrinsically known how to banish the quiddity from the Harlop Estate even before she had been shown how.

The gap in her childhood was so very much like Robert's that it was incredible that she hadn't noticed the similarities before.

Or maybe she *had* noticed them, but had blocked these painful memories deep down inside.

Shelly thought back to when they were in the helicopter, when she had been mostly asleep and had hollered after Robert when he ran toward Seaforth Prison.

"I know."

Why did I say that? Why?

Tears spilled down her cheeks and dripped onto the photograph. They distorted the much younger version of herself sitting on the church floor, which was only fitting, given how she felt right now. It was as if her life had been ripped out from beneath her.

A series of images flooded her mind then, materializing slowly at first but quickly picking up steam. She saw her foster parents, their kind, loving faces, their laughs. Then she was transported backwards in time, and now she was the girl in the photo, sitting on the floor of the church, waiting for Father Callahan to come collect her. Next, she was at the massive wooden church doors, a man holding her hand, offering her to the priest. The flashes of her past started to speed up, moving backward, culminating in the image of a drab classroom, of plain desks. Of dust motes circling in stale air.

She was a Guardian, she knew that with as much conviction as she knew she was pregnant. She had been there, in the orphanage, when it had all begun. Before...

Shelly closed her eyes tightly, trying to remember, while at the same time hoping that she couldn't. Something horrible had happened at that orphanage, something that had left many of them dead. But try as she might, she couldn't recall any of the details. The crappy desks, the drab classroom, candles flickering across scared faces; she remembered all of these things. She remembered the teachings, bits and pieces of someone instructing her—*them*—and it dawned on her that this was likely why she had been so adamant about denying the existence of the book, *Inter vivos et mortuos*.

Because the mental block that had been erected in her mind had convinced her that it didn't exist—that that *time* didn't exist. It couldn't exist, as nothing that bad, that horrible, could happen to children.

That life was not *her*.

Shelly suddenly felt pity for Robert, for what he must have gone through when he'd had the rug had been pulled out from beneath him.

For what he must have felt upon realizing that everything he'd thought about where he had come from, who he was, had been just a lie, perpetrated by Father Callahan and Sean Sommers.

And Robert wasn't the only one.

The orphanage, I need to get to the orphanage. There are answers there.

Shelly wiped the tears from her cheeks and put the photograph in her pocket. She felt movement in her belly, and she put her hand there, expecting to feel the baby kick.

But it was too early for that.

It was probably only indigestion.

And then she did the very thing she had promised herself she would never do. Shelly ran down the stairs, threw the massive door open, and shouted into the night.

"Robert! Robert, get the fuck back here! I'm sorry! *I didn't know!*"

But the only answer was the wind and the chirping of a blackbird embedded in the dark sky.

Sobbing now, overcome by emotion and hormonal changes, Shelly went back inside the Estate where she grabbed a pencil and a piece of paper and began writing.

Chapter 27

"WELL? WHAT ARE WE going to do now? Just sit and wait for the FBI to arrive?" Bella demanded.

Carson looked at Michael, who was staring out of the crematorium door at the eight dead bodies that stood awaiting further instruction. There was a drop of blood in the corner of his mouth, and his lower lip was circumscribed by a dark red line.

"One; one FBI agent. What did the older detective say the man's name was?"

"Agent Brett Cherry," Michael responded, not taking his eyes away from the dead. Carson didn't blame him.

"Yeah, that's right. Agent Cherry."

"We can't just keep the two detectives in the back of the truck forever, you know," Bella piped in.

"I know."

"Do you know where they parked their car?" Michael asked.

"I thought you said they came in the truck?"

"They did. But if they just grabbed Vinny close to here and hopped in, that means their car is nearby. Every one of those damn police cars has GPS—if the two detectives don't check in after a certain period of time, they're going to trace them here. And then we are going to have a much bigger problem to deal with than one FBI agent."

Carson scratched his chin.

"Where is that cocksucker Vinny, anyway? You said he went inside?"

"I said I *think* he went inside. Detectives ambushed me and I didn't see where he went."

Carson turned to Bella.

"Take a peek around, see if you can find him."

Bella glared at him; she wasn't the type of woman that took kindly to being told what to do. Not by Carson, not by anyone.

"What about him?" she asked, gesturing to Michael, who didn't notice as his eyes were still staring at the twitching dead.

"What about him?"

"Why doesn't he look for Vinny?"

Carson chuckled.

"Because he'll eat him, that's why."

At the mention of eating, Michael craned his neck around.

"You said I could have him."

"And now I changed my mind. You could've had him, but you fucked up by letting the cops get the jump on you."

Michael turned to face him completely, his finger aimed at the center of his chest, a scowl on his face.

"I fucked up? *I* fucked up?"

"Well, yeah. You fucked up."

Michael took a step forward, and Bella instantly slid to flank him.

"I was up here hauling bodies, while you two were downstairs doing your hippie bullshit. And that Vinny guy? *You* were the one who told him to get more bodies; I wanted to kill him on the spot."

Carson chewed the inside of his lip, but before he could answer, Michael took another aggressive step forward.

"What's your master plan, Carson? Care to fill me in? Because"—he gestured to the dead twitching outside in the mud—"while this is all pretty fucking fascinating, I was doing quite fine by myself before you arrived on the scene. So? What's next? We go after Robert again? Get him to open the rift?"

Carson didn't say anything for several seconds. He hadn't had the chance to share with Bella what his father had told him, and he'd wanted to let her in on it before Michael found out.

But now it looked like that wasn't possible.

He sighed.

"These aren't enough. And besides, I don't think that I need Robert anymore."

Bella gawked at him.

"Wait? Not enough? What about the others in the basement? That makes, what? Eighteen? Nineteen?"

"Twenty," Carson corrected her. He shook his head. "But it's still not enough."

Michael scoffed.

"How many do you need? An army?"

Carson smiled, even though he felt as if he had had this discussion before. Soon, it would be time to share everything he knew, and when that time came, both Bella and Michael would understand. But until then, they were just going to have to trust him.

Trust him and listen to him.

"Yeah, something like that. Or maybe just better soldiers."

***

Bella moved swiftly down the stairs, her feet barely grazing each step before moving on to the next.

Vinny was down here, she just knew he was. The man was a lurking, spindly bastard who knew nothing but his job. He wouldn't leave Scarsdale, no matter what he saw or what happened here. Shit, the man hadn't even asked where Jonah was, and he was probably the closest thing that Vinny had had to a friend.

No, he was here somewhere. He couldn't leave this place.

As Bella made her way into the basement, her eyes darting about the dim space, she mulled over what Carson had said upstairs.

We need to go to an orphanage. Sacred Heart Orphanage.

Bella had gone along with him up to this point, but she feared for the man's sanity now, especially after how deep he had gone during their last session.

She hadn't told him, but he had been seizing just prior to waking and he had stopped breathing. Not for long, but long enough to make it clear that any deeper and he likely wouldn't make it back.

And then there was the issue of the bodies...how could twenty dead bodies not be enough? Robert had had a hard enough time keeping just eight of them at bay back at the Estate. And now that they were aware of his little talent, they wouldn't be taken by surprise again.

That was the worst of it; Bella *hated* being taken by surprise. She had even hated Carson creeping up on her at the *Panty Snatcher*, but she had given him a pass.

No, this time she wouldn't be taken by surprise. This time, *they* would be the ones doing the surprising.

An orphanage.

Clearly, Carson hadn't told her everything that Leland had shared with him, otherwise she would've known what the fuck the big deal was with an abandoned orphanage.

Back when they had met, all those years ago, she had fallen for him quickly. He wasn't a normal man, and his brain didn't function as a normal man's might. At first she'd thought that he was just a demented psychopath like all the rest, but when she had started to interview him, to listen to what he was actually saying, she'd known he was different.

Only a young boy then, he'd had insights into the human condition that far exceeded his age or his experience.

And then there was the Marrow.

A sound to Bella's left suddenly drew her attention. She had purposely kept the basement dark, so as to better hone her other senses. The eyes, she had found, were the most easily misled, often commandeered by emotions, thoughts, feelings.

The sound was a nearly inaudible intake of breath. Its location was indistinct, but had a slight echo to it.

Bella silently slid to her right, picking up the opaqueness of an object directly in front of her. She put her hand out, and laid it on the clay tile. Then she listened.

Sure enough, she could hear someone breathing.

A smile crossed her face as she realized what her hand was touching.

The oven.

Vinny, that fucking half-wit, had decided to hide inside the oven.

I love being right—this is the only thing that the man knows. I knew he wouldn't leave here.

Detecting no change in the breathing pattern, she slipped to one side, feeling her way along the hard exterior, all the while Carson's words repeated in her mind.

If you find him, leave him for Michael. He's earned a little snack, and an ear ain't gonna cut it...am I right, Michael? But not enough to kill him...just a snack.

Her hand found something jutting from the ceramic surface.

Well, fuck it, I deserve something, too.

A smile crossed her pretty face as she reared back and jammed her palm against the button.

Her vision was suddenly filled with the glow of a fire.

A second later, the screams started.

Chapter 28

"**WHAT THE FUCK ARE** you talking about?" Robert demanded.

Sean eyed the man standing across from him.

"Please, Robert. I've read the book—I fucking read that book cover to cover so many times I know it by heart. You have to trust me, the boo—"

"Trust you? *Trust* you? Ever since I first met you, you've been lying or deceiving or keeping something from me. Why in God's name would I trust you now?"

Sean bowed his head.

"I know, Robert, I know. I haven't been honest to you from the get-go. But you have to understand, I couldn't tell you everything; I just couldn't."

Robert threw his hands up.

"Why not? Jesus fucking Christ, why can't you just tell the truth for once, Sean? Why do you have to drop breadcrumbs—Ruth Harlop is my aunt, fucking Leland is my father, he needs Amy to open the rift, oh, not Amy, but Shelly's baby—what the fuck!"

Sean was curious about Robert's choice of words—*Shelly's baby*—but filed this away for later.

"I couldn't tell you because the Cloak wouldn't let me, that's why."

Robert turned his back to Sean, his frustration reaching a head.

"The Cloak? *Cloak?* Cal, you ever heard of the Cloak?"

Cal shrugged.

"The Cloak sounds like something from *The Skulls*...or it's just some made-up bullshit by a man who is desperate to save his own life."

Sean shook his head.

"Aiden?"

Aiden hesitated before answering, and Sean glared at him. Just a few days ago, Aiden had been one of his best men, if not *the* best, an ex-military dynamo that followed his every order. The man hadn't even batted an eyelash when Sean had told him that they were going to break into a maximum-security prison. But now...

But now Aiden was dead, as fucked up as that sounded. Dead and still here. Which meant that Leland and his felonious son were building strength.

And that was a real concern.

And then there was Aiden's new attitude. That was also a major problem. But if Sean had any say in it, it wouldn't be an issue for long.

"Aiden, please tell them about the Cloak."

Aiden spat on the floor.

"Don't know much, but Sean is telling the truth; from my observations, he seemed to be taking orders from someone. I saw a person once, small, feminine. Wore a cloak."

Feminine?

"Look, Robert, we need to hurry. Leland can track you—you know this."

He caught Robert take a quick glance down to his calf.

"Please, there isn't much time."

As Sean watched, Robert grabbed Cal's arm and pulled him close. They exchanged whispers, and then Robert turned back to him, a frown on his face.

"Alright, I'll play your fucking game. Let's go see your contact, but when we're done, you tell us where Carson is."

Sean nodded vigorously.

"Yes, yes, please—it's a deal."

"And I get to keep the book."

Sean swore.

"No. I can't—"

"Carson and the book or no deal."

He closed his eyes, and pictured the rough leather cover in his mind. After a few moments, he realized that his fingers were moving, tracing the embossed letters—*Inter vivos et mortuos*—on the imaginary cover. He couldn't let it go; *wouldn't* let it go.

"Fine," he lied. "Just get me the fuck out of here."

Robert nodded, then gestured for Aiden to step forward.

"We are not fucking around, Sean. I get one whiff of you holding back or trying something and Aiden here is going to give you a big ol' fucking bear hug, you understand?"

Sean nodded again, his arms tensing against the ropes that bound him.

"Yes, yes, I understand."

But when the Cloak hears what I have to say, even Aiden—dead or alive—won't be able to save you.

***

"I don't think this is a good idea," Cal whispered to Robert. Even though his head was covered again, Sean could make out the words just fine. "It could be a trick."

There was a pause.

"He won't say anything if we don't take him—I saw it in his eyes."

"Yeah, but where's the guarantee that he'll say anything after we take him? Huh, Robbo?"

Another pause, and the car ran over a bump of some sort, jostling Sean. He kept as close as possible to the door on his right to avoid touching Aiden, who was sitting beside him in the backseat with only the one empty spot between them.

"Hey, shithead? You sure it's here? This fucking tower? Looks like an office building to me."

Sean cleared his throat.

"The Trellis Tower?"

"Yep," Cal answered quickly. "We're here."

"Good, good, this is it. Now let me out, I need to—"

"No chance," Robert cut him off, bringing the car to a stop. "You tell us how to communicate with the Cloak, and he comes down here."

Sean shook his head, the thick fabric bag scratching his cheeks and nose.

"He never leaves. He's always up there, in the room on the top floor. Room 21. And he won't answer to you guys, only to me."

Sean felt the pressure change and cool air hit his arms as someone opened his door. Hands slipped under his armpits and he was yanked out of the vehicle. Disoriented, he nearly fell backwards, but someone pushed him from behind and he straightened. A moment later, the hood was unceremoniously pulled off his head.

Sean blinked quickly, trying to force his eyes to adjust to the dim light. They were in a nearly empty parking lot, in front of Trellis Tower, a tall, jet-black edifice that extended into the night sky. It was a building he was familiar with, partly because it was where the Seaforth board members met, but mainly because this was the only place that the Cloak would see him.

"This is it," he whispered. His heart was racing in his chest. *The child of two Guardians...*

"Yeah, this is it. So now what? You have some secret code or something to get in? Keys on a large brass ring, maybe?"

Sean turned to face Cal, and immediately frowned when he saw that Aiden was standing behind him, his arms crossed over his chest, his rifle still strapped to his back.

How long can he stay here before the Marrow tries to reel him in?

"Eh, Sean!" Cal snapped his fingers. "Wake up! I asked you how you get in. You have keys?"

Sean shook his head and shrugged his tense shoulders.

"Untie me," he instructed, looking to Robert.

"No chance."

Sean ground his teeth in frustration.

"Fine," he said, stomping toward the front entrance. Cal followed closely behind, while Robert stepped beside him. He assumed that Aiden took up the rear, but didn't actually see the man move.

"You shouldn't be here," he said to Robert as they approached the door. "None of you should be here. You should be with Shelly. If Carson..." He let his sentence trail off, scolding himself for running his mouth again.

"If Carson what?" Robert demanded.

"Nothing." Sean indicated the keypad with his chin. "There."

Robert suddenly grabbed him by the shoulders and Sean was whipped around. The man's eyes were red and there were heavy bags hanging beneath them.

"That is why we need to find him before he finds us," he hissed. "And you're going to help us."

Sean swallowed hard.

Robert wasn't seeing it.

"Fine." He again signaled the keypad. "Punch in 212121."

When Robert just kept his gaze locked, Cal stepped forward and punched in the code.

Robert was blinded, wasn't seeing the truth; the fact that if there was *no* baby, then the rift could never be opened at all.

"Yes," the intercom squawked. The voice was haggard to begin with, but through the intercom it was nearly unrecognizable as human. Sean caught Robert and Cal exchange a look. He stepped forward.

"It's Sean. I need to come up, and I'm not alone."

Chapter 29

"YOU WERE THERE, WEREN'T you? At Seaforth?" Ben asked quietly. He kicked at the sand beneath his feet.

Allan nodded.

"I was there, I saw."

Ben sighed and shook his head.

"All of my men, dead. And Father Callahan, he was killed too." He fought back tears. "All on my watch. My watch…"

Ben bowed his head. A second later, he gasped when the boy's arms wrapped around him. His first instinct was to pull away, but he was too tired for that. Too tired and just too damn sad. Ben had to lean down, but when he did, he started sobbing into the boy's shoulder like a baby.

For some time, he just cried; he cried for as long as the images of his men hanging in the mess hall, of Quinn with his eyes torn out, with Callahan split in half, that horrible light coming through his chest, remained a fixture in his mind.

And of him falling, endlessly falling, only to splash into lukewarm water.

When these images finally faded, he raised his head and wiped his face. The boy's shoulder was soaked from his tears.

"Sorry," he managed to croak, his throat dry.

Allan nodded.

"I've lost, too. I know how it feels."

Ben looked skyward to the glowing sun above, then turned his attention to the strange, symmetrical waves.

"What is this place? Is it Heaven? Hell? Purgatory?"

When Allan didn't respond, Ben lowered his head. The boy had walked forward several feet.

"You know, don't you? It's that place that Father Callahan mentioned. The one that…" He felt tears coming again, spurred by just the thought of his old friend.

The friend that he hadn't listened to, that he had thought a fool.

"What is this place?" he asked again, his voice barely a whisper. He picked up his pace to come up next to Allan.

The boy's head was down, his footsteps lethargic.

"It's called the Marrow," he said at last. "It's where everyone goes when they die."

Ben swallowed hard.

He knew that he was dead, had known it the moment that the man in the blood-covered suit had tripped him and he had fallen into the hole in Callahan's chest. And yet hearing the boy say those words brought them into focus. Made them real.

Made this whole situation real.

And Ben couldn't help the feelings of pity and sorrow that came over him.

He had led a good life, but it had ended just so wrong. It couldn't be the end; he couldn't let his friends' deaths go unpunished.

He just couldn't do it.

So many men dead…good men, men with families, with —

"All of the dead come here," Allan said, interrupting his thoughts. He stopped abruptly, and Ben followed his gaze over the waves. For a few seconds, that was all Ben saw. But the longer he stared, the more he thought he could make out something in the distance. It was a small, dark speck on the horizon, but goddamn him if he didn't think it was some sort of island.

"The dead come here and are put to a decision."

Ben nodded, recalling what Father Callahan had said what felt like a million years ago back at Seaforth.

He waited for Allan to continue, but when he looked over and saw that he was crying now, silent tears making tracks on his dirty face, he reached for the boy and wrapped his arm around his shoulder.

It was his turn to console.

"And have you decided what you're going to do?"

Lightning suddenly cracked, and the sky started to darken as if a tropical storm was brewing.

Instead of answering, Allan flipped the question back to him.

"Have you?"

Chapter 30

"YOU CAN'T BE SERIOUS," the Cloak croaked.

Sean shrugged.

"I had no choice."

The man pulled the cloak down low, hiding his face completely. But despite not being able to see him, Sean knew that he was seeing them.

"You brought Robert here?"

"How do you know who I am?" Robert suddenly spoke up. He tried to squeeze by Sean, to get in front of him, but the Cloak held up a hand and he came to a stop.

"And a quiddity? You brought a quiddity *here*? Do you not feel that in your chest, Sean? Do you not know that there is something else going on?"

Sean, head bowed, answered.

"I had no choice. I have...I have *learned* something, something important, and I need to see the book."

The Cloak scoffed.

"You *need* to do your job as a Guardian, Sean. You need to keep the Marrow safe. That is what you need to do. You don't need to come here, to bring the dead here. I don't care what kind of shit you've gotten yourself into."

Sean's head snapped up. The time for obsequious metaphors had passed.

"Carson isn't dead. He's alive. And Amy isn't the girl that Leland needs, it's Shelly's unborn baby."

This time it was the Cloak who stopped in his tracks.

***

Sean rubbed his sore shoulders, grimacing at the tension that had built up after being bound for what felt like hours. Then he put his hands on the table in front of him. All five of them were in the room, Cal, the Cloak, Robert, Sean, and Aiden, only Aiden was standing at the back of the room while the rest of them were seated at the table.

The Cloak had the *Inter vivos* out in front of him, the pages open to a passage that both he and Sean knew well.

"A Guardian, bound between worlds, will open the rift, but the Guardian won't be able to hold it open. Only the quiddity of a child, of a powerful child born of two Guardians, will be able to hold it open and allow souls to flow backward into the world of the living."

"Are you sure that's what it says?" Sean asked, leaning forward.

The Cloak hesitated before answering.

"This is my translation. I don't know if the Keeper had another one."

"He did," Robert answered, and surprised that he had spoken, Sean turned towards him. Robert, however, had his eyes locked on the book. "I know he did."

"How come we didn't realize this before?" the Cloak demanded.

Sean shrugged.

"I don't know; maybe because he already had Amy, that's the child we assumed he needed?" At the mention of his daughter's name, a pained expression crossed over Robert's face. Sean ignored it and continued, "But it makes sense, the power of two Guardians...has there ever been such a person? A child born of two Guardians?"

The cloak shifted back and forth; he was shaking his head.

"I still can't believe that Shelly is a Guardian," Robert whispered. Out of the corner of his eye, Sean saw Cal reach over and comfort him. It bothered him that Cal was tagging along; the man was a mess, driven by motives that for whatever reason Rob was blind to. He wasn't a Guardian, he had no business being here.

His eyes flicked up to Aiden.

And *he* shouldn't have been here at all.

"First things first," the Cloak rasped. "Robert, is your brother still alive?"

Robert bowed his head before answering.

"I couldn't kill him," he whispered. "That would make me the same as him, and I'm not him. I'm not *that*."

Sean's eyes narrowed as he recalled Robert putting a bullet in Callahan's head.

You are more like him than you think.

The thought was sudden, instinctive, and it startled Sean.

It also scared him, as the more he thought about it, the more it rang true. Then he came back to what the cloaked one had said long ago, that the world might be better without Guardians. That without Guardians, there could be no rifts. And without a powerful child, the Marrow would remain a one-way street forever.

"That's okay, Robert. I understand. And Shelly, you're sure she's pregnant?"

Robert nodded.

Sean was having a hard time understanding the Cloak's reaction to it all; he had expected outrage, a violent display, perhaps, but what he detected was something akin to compassion.

They didn't have time for this.

"I think—" he began, but the Cloak held up a hand, stopping him mid-sentence.

"Why did you allow them to come together? You know how important it is to keep them apart, don't you? How can you forget what happened with Leland?"

Before Sean could answer, to espouse his innocence, to remind the Cloak that he hadn't known that Shelly was a Guardian, that he had somehow forgotten, something in his mind clicked.

Something about the orphanage, about him saving three children, instead of just two.

It was as if misty condensation had settled on his neurons back around the time when Leland had started gaining power, when Ruth Harlop and her family had hung around for far too long. But now that the fog had been lifted, he realized that Leland was somehow scrambling all of their thoughts, which would explain why Robert knew nothing about when Sean dropped him off at the church, or his time at the orphanage before that.

Sean swallowed hard, wondering what else Leland held power over.

"Leland...what happened to him? How did he die?" Robert shot a look over at Sean, and he knew that the man was recalling what he had admitted at Seaforth.

That he had killed Leland.

And it was true.

But Robert didn't know the half of it, and if it were up to him, it would stay that way.

"Another time, Robert. But for now, we have one job to do. We have to find Shelly," the Cloak interceded.

Robert made a face.

"Find her? She's back at the Estate. She wasn't...she wasn't feeling well, from the pregnancy. What we need to do is to find

Carson, and do what I should have done back at the prison. We need to take him out so that we can be free again."

The Cloak didn't answer for a long time. When he did, his voice was even more gruff than it had been moments ago.

"She's not at the Estate anymore."

"She's not? She—"

"Look inside, Robert. You are a Guardian. Look deep, deep inside."

Sean saw the man's face contort, but to his surprise instead of answering back, Robert remained silent and shut his eyes.

A moment later, they popped open again.

"Sacred Heart Orphanage," he said almost robotically. "She went to Sacred Heart Orphanage."

Cal let out his breath in a *whoosh.*

"What? Where? Is she—is she okay?"

Robert nodded, but it was the Cloak who responded for him.

"She's fine, for now. But I fear that she is on a collision course with Carson."

Cal's face went white and he shot to his feet.

"Well what the fuck are we waiting for? Let's get the hell out of here!"

The Cloak also rose, and Sean noticed for the first time just how stooped he was. And short; the Cloak was only about five foot four, he realized.

"Yes, we must hurry."

Sean was taken aback by this. For as long as he had known the Cloak, one of the original Guardians, he had never left the Trellis Tower.

"You're coming?" he nearly gasped.

The Cloak nodded.

"I have no choice. The barrier is weakening, and I fear this is our last chance to stop the rift from opening."

PART III - Sacred, Broken Hearts and Family Values

Chapter 31

AGENT BRETT CHERRY BROUGHT the flask to his mouth and took a sip. It was sour, horrible stuff, but he forced it down anyway, wiping the small amount that rested on his lip with the back of his hand.

Then he tossed the silver flask onto the passenger seat and turned his eyes back to the road. He burped and squinted hard before stretching his eyebrows upward. His forehead was stiff and sore.

It was nearly dusk, but the sun was still too bright for Agent Cherry, given the bender he had been on lately. He hadn't even wanted to wake up this morning, and probably wouldn't have, if Ed the Nose hadn't called him. It had been so long since he had heard from his old friend that when he had said who it was, Agent Cherry hadn't even believed him at first.

To Brett, reality had undergone a shift ever since his partner, Agent Kendra Wilson, had been so horribly murdered in the swamp. Before that time, he'd thought he had a grip on reality, that he knew the rules.

That he knew what he was doing.

But that was not the world that he existed in now. He had seen the blackened thing on the ground, the one with the glowing initials JB on her back. He had seen the dead, the evil in this world, and it had changed him.

A shudder ran through Brett, and he immediately grabbed for the flask.

And then the girls...all of those girls shouting the same thing over and over and over again.

Enter me! Enter me! Enter me!

Brett closed his eyes and took a good, long swig.

No, today, like everyday since Kendra's murder, he definitely hadn't wanted to wake up.

For a sweet second, he kept his eyes closed, debating whether or not he should just keep driving on the country road, just let go of everything and allow his car to drift where it wanted.

His foot pressed the accelerator just a little harder as his car started to veer to one side. The front tire hit something hard and jolted his eyes open. There was a tree, a thick oak tree, at the side of the road only about forty feet from where he was now.

It would be so easy just to swerve into it, smash into it.

To end it all.

No one would blame him.

"Fuck," he swore, righting the wheel and putting the car back on the road. "Fuck, fuck, fuck."

In the distance, he saw the sign for the crematorium. Even from a few miles down the road, the sight of the building accosted him like some sort of foul smell.

The sign looked like the advertisement for a haunted house, the curly 's' of 'Scarsdale' twisting down into a snake, the wooden frame showing in several places where the decal had worn thin.

On top of the dark blue placard, another sign had been hastily stuck, but had since started peeling at the corners.

No visitors.

In the distance, he saw a square, gray building with a large chimney jutting from the flat roof like a single buck tooth.

A thick cloud of black smoke billowed from the tooth, which Brett thought of as a good sign. A sign that meant someone was here.

Ed the Nose.

His detective friend hadn't even needed to tell him what he was calling about; Brett knew it from his voice. It was about the Michael Young case, the sicko from NYC who liked to eat women alive.

Brett was familiar with the case. His boss, Director Ames, had told him to be on alert, that he might have to go into the field, as much as the man knew it would pain Brett to do so without Kendra at his side.

But his friend needed help, backup, and so now he was here.

Brett knew that Ed was planning an ambush, but he had said that if he didn't hear back from him by four, to head on over. Considering that Brett had already flown in from South Carolina, it was only a short drive to the crematorium.

A quick glance at the dashboard revealed that it was already a quarter to five, and his foot pressed down on the accelerator. A few minutes later, he pulled his rented Chevy right up to the front doors, noting the deep grooves in the mud.

Then he drew his gun and stepped out into the fading sun.

***

Scarsdale Crematorium was empty, save the still smoldering body in the oven. But someone had been here recently — several people, in fact. While there were no signs of struggle, and the place was generally a dump, he noted several different footprints on the dusty floor.

And it reeked of death.

Brett hesitated, trying to figure out what to do next. He had already called Ed, but it had gone straight to voicemail. He had called the precinct as well, but the dispatcher had informed him that Ed and his partner Hugh had gone out that morning and hadn't returned.

Brett peeked into the oven again and his heart skipped a beat. The body was charred, a blackened, crispy mess that was only distinguishably human by the outline.

And for the briefest of moments, he thought it was Kendra, her lipless mouth forming a horrible kissy face.

"You let me burn, Brett," he heard in his head. Or at least he thought it was in his head. *"You were supposed to save me, but instead you just fucked me and then left me to burn."*

Brett's eyes started to water, but he gritted his teeth and tried not to break down again. He wished he had his flask with him and not back in the car.

After all, that was what the alcohol was for: to forget, to numb, to not feel.

He hurried back up the stairs, coughing and spitting a black smear of saliva on the floor. When he made it to the top step, he took out his phone and dialed the last name on his rather short mental rolodex.

"Yeah, Director Ames. I'm here. Ed isn't."

There was a pause, and for a second Brett thought that maybe the phone had gone dead—reception had been sporadic ever since he had started down the dirt road. But then the director spoke in the same monotone voice he always used.

"Brett, I've received word that Michael is headed to Sacred Heart Orphanage."

Brett screwed up his face.

"Received word? From who? Did Ed call you?"

Another pause.

"You need to head to the orphanage. Keep your eyes and ears peeled. You are to do recon and call me once you get there, got it? For no reason are you to interact with anyone you see at the orphanage, Ed, Hugh, and Michael included. You got it?"

Brett pushed a thumb and forefinger into his eyes.

He had not been expecting this.

Not supposed to interact? Even with Ed?

"What's going on, Ames? What the fuck is going on? Is this related to Kendra somehow?"

The man ignored his question.

"Do you understand, Brett?"

"Fuck," he whispered under his breath. "Yeah, I understand. Send the directions to my phone and I'll head over there. What's the place called again?"

This time, the response was immediate.

"Sacred Heart Orphanage. And Brett?"

"Yeah?"

"Do. Not. Engage."

Chapter 32

THERE WAS SOMETHING ABOUT the man in the cloak that Robert found oddly familiar, but like many things in his life—his *new* life—he couldn't quite place the feeling.

He had enough trouble getting his mind around the idea that Shelly was a Guardian, that she was pregnant, that Sean had brought them to this high-rise office building, the Trellis Tower.

And that Shelly and his baby were in danger.

The man in the cloak slipped the book into his robe, and then dialed a number on his cell phone as they made their way toward the elevator.

Seeing that worn leather cover again incited a strong desire in Robert to reach out and grab the book, but he forced it away. With all of this talk about his unborn child, it seemed that everyone had forgotten about Amy.

But he hadn't.

His goal was still to get her back.

The man in the cloak grumbled something that he didn't quite pick up, then he ended the call.

Cal, on the other hand, had heard something, and it piqued his interest.

"FBI? You called the FBI about this?"

The Cloak raised his chin, and Robert realized that it wasn't just a cloak that he was wearing, but there was some sort of black mask or turtleneck covering his face as well.

Who the fuck is this guy?

Sean had described him as one of the original Guardians, one of the most powerful, but that meant little to Robert.

Where did the Guardians come from? When did they come from?

"There is so much that you don't know, Cal. There are people in high places that are aware of the Marrow and the imminent danger, and who can help us if we really need it."

Instead of being reassured, Cal threw his hands up in frustration.

"I'm sick and tired of people telling me that I don't know nothing. Well, shit, if the leader of The Skulls would just *tell* me something, then maybe you can save your fucking breath later on. You know, an investment in your future."

Robert reached out and placed a hand on his friend's shoulder, trying to calm him. He half-expected Cal to pull away, but the man didn't. Instead, he actually leaned into him.

"You have a car?" Robert asked.

The Cloak shook his head.

"Mine is here," Sean informed them.

Robert mulled this over. He still loathed the man for being a cold-blooded murderer, for using poor Allan and Cal as bait, for getting him involved in all of this mess, despite the fact that he seemed genuinely concerned for both Shelly and the unborn baby's safety.

"Cal, you go with Aiden, and I'll go with Sean and the Cloak."

Cal shook his head.

"No fucking way; we go together—we're in this together, we fucking ride together."

Robert mulled this over. He had wanted time alone with the Cloak, to see if he could somehow get his hands on the book, but Cal was probably right.

It was best if they stuck together.

He turned to Sean.

"How big is your car?"

"I have an SUV, seven-seater."

"Perfect. We'll take that, then."

***

"It's an hour drive to Sacred Heart," Robert informed them, peering up from his phone. "So I think that the time will be best served telling us what you know."

Sean, who was in the driver seat, turned to him.

"I told you already, you —"

"Aiden here thinks that you should start speaking, too, or he starts doling out hugs," Cal offered.

The Cloak, who was in the passenger seat, turned and cast a glance at Aiden, who was in the third row of the SUV. Although Robert couldn't see his eyes, he somehow knew that, unlike Sean, this one had no fear of the dead.

"You want to know about Leland?" the man demanded with his scratchy voice.

Robert nodded.

"For starters."

Sean shot a look over at the Cloak, but it was obvious even to Robert who was the subordinate here. As uncomfortable as he looked, there was no way that he was going to challenge the Cloak.

The man sighed heavily.

"Leland Black is the embodiment of pure evil, a coalescence of all of the most primal of emotions: lust, anger, pain, love, all of these wrapped up into an idea of a human being. He wasn't always this way, but a long time ago, something happened to him, something that changed him. You see, some people are selfish, obsessed with the self, with the idea of being unique. But we aren't unique; *humans* aren't unique. We are but worker bees in possession of a hive mind. The idea of self-awareness is just a blip, an evolutionary mistake, one that makes us think that there is such thing as a *self*."

Robert tried to wrap his mind around this idea; it was one that he had heard before, but he had yet to fully come to terms with it. And it was his brother, Carson Black of all people, who had first spouted this rhetoric.

No self? How can that be? I am...I am me, *aren't I?*

"Think of Leland as the id, without the protecting oversight of the ego. He truly is evil, and believes that by opening the rift, by proving to everyone that dying isn't just a one-way street, that he can transform this Earth. In reality, however, if he succeeds, he will destroy it."

Robert looked over at Cal, who was staring so intently that there were creases forming all over his forehead.

"The thing about Leland," the Cloak continued, clearing his voice, "is that he has harnessed the power of the Marrow, powers that no man should be in possession of. And it has changed him even further. Now when you look at Leland, you see your greatest fear embodied."

"Wait, what?" Cal asked.

Robert was also incredulous. He swallowed hard, remembering the horror of seeing Leland lift his head, of showing him his face.

And that face had been Robert's.

What the hell does it mean?

"Leland embodies your fear, latches on to it and uses it to control you. The most susceptible are the insecure, the outcasts, the evil ones themselves."

"Like Jonah and Michael," Cal whispered.

The Cloak ignored the comment, but Robert was thinking the same thing.

"The Marrow must remain closed. The evil harbored therein must stay locked away. We have to do everything in our power to keep it that way. It is our duty as Guardians."

Robert was suddenly sweating, and he wiped it from his brow. He licked his tacky lower lip and then turned to look at Aiden, who was staring out the window. He wondered what the man was thinking, given that he was dead.

"What do you see when you look at him?" Robert nearly gasped. "What do you see?"

The Cloak turned his gaze back to the windshield without saying anything. The pause went on for so long that Robert thought the man was going to refrain entirely.

But then he spoke, and his words took Robert's breath away.

"I see you, Robert. I see your face."

Robert started to tremble, and he pictured not him, but this man in the cloak, this small man with the stooped spine and the gravelly voice, on the beach approaching the Goat.

And then looking up and seeing Robert's face beneath that wide-brimmed hat.

Helen, who had been quiet for so long that Robert had almost forgotten that she was in his head, finally spoke up.

But what she said wasn't anything that Robert expected.

He's a woman.

"What?" he whispered out loud. Cal shot him a glance, but he ignored it.

Look at the way she moves, the small hands. The Cloak isn't a man; it's a woman.

Robert stared at the cloaked person in front of him, trying to observe his mannerisms, his posture.

You know what? he thought. *I think you're right.*

But that didn't change the fact that Robert himself was the woman's greatest fear.

Chapter 33

"WHAT ARE WE DOING here, Carson?" Michael asked, his voice dripping with annoyance. Carson didn't answer right away. Instead, he simply gazed out of the window at the massive brick structure before them.

It had been a time since he had been to Sacred Heart Orphanage. A long, *long* time. Back then, he had been but a child, learning the details of the Marrow, of the afterlife that he would soon thereafter abandon.

It was even before Sean had taken him to the church. Father Callahan's church.

A smile crossed his face as he remembered the man spread eagle on the floor of his cell. The priest deserved that. After all, he had let him go; he was to blame for Sean leaving him with those horrible junkie stepparents.

Carson shook his head, and looked at the place. There were souls here, dead souls. *Important* dead souls.

Young, but powerful.

His patented Cheshire grin began to form on his thin lips.

"Carson? I asked what we're doing here."

Carson turned, but instead of offering a response, he looked at Bella first.

"Open the back of the truck, get things ready."

Bella nodded, and immediately pulled her door open. Although she hated being ordered around, he could tell that she felt the power of this place.

She knew what was at stake.

Carson turned to Michael next.

"This isn't going to be easy, Michael—we're going to need your help."

Michael's expression soured.

"Help with what? It seems all I've been doing is helping you and your girlfriend, but I am getting nothing out of it."

Carson's smile grew.

Michael reminded him of a much younger version of himself, despite the fact that the man was older than he was.

"Today is a glorious day, Michael. Today, Daddy's coming home."

***

The halls were empty, seemingly undisturbed since the last time anyone had been in the orphanage.

Since Carson himself had been in there.

There were still dark streaks of blood on the floor, long tracks of the dried liquid marking the hallways.

Back then, no one had known that they were even here, so no one had known to clean up after them. And the kids had already been lost souls, so there'd been no one to look for them, either.

As Carson made his way down the hallway, he tried to ignore the dust that his footsteps made airborne.

"Keep walking," he instructed Ed and Hugh, who not only had their hands bound behind their backs, but were also tied to each other.

The men shuffled forward, and Carson looked around. Bella was on one side, Michael on the other. The twenty dead souls that he had ordered into the back of the truck were treading behind them like some sort of winding worm.

The smile that had formed on Carson's face in the truck remained plastered on his face. Despite what had happened at Seaforth, things were looking up.

Leland was ready, and Carson almost had everything he needed to bring him home.

They continued to make their way down the main hall, and while it looked like Carson was just wandering aimlessly, he wasn't.

He knew exactly where he was going.

They passed several old-fashioned classrooms, and Carson went over to one of them and peered through the dusty glass.

"No," he muttered. "Not this one."

They passed two more, identical to the first. When they came to the fourth window, something in Carson's chest started to tighten. He didn't need to see the brown stains covering the concrete just outside the door to know that this was the right one.

"This is the room," he said. "Michael, open the door and lead our guests in. This is the spot."

He couldn't keep the excitement from his voice. As Michael led Ed and Hugh into the room, Bella pulled him close.

"Are you sure this is going to work? I mean, they've been dead for so long...haven't they passed over already?"

Carson shook his head.

"They aren't normal kids, Bella. They are Guardians. They don't follow the same rules as everyone else...which is why Leland has been able to stay on the shores for so long."

Bella's face was smooth, soft, and Carson leaned down and kissed her on the lips.

"It's going to happen this time, Bella. I know it is." He put a finger to his chest. "I can feel it."

He also knew that if his plan worked, then it would create such an energy pulse that all of the remaining Guardians would feel it. And the bastards would have no choice but to come. And when they did, Carson and his army would be waiting.

"Go on in," he instructed, and Bella entered with Carson following closely after. Once inside, he surveyed the room.

It was much how he remembered it from all those years ago. The simple, wooden desks, the chalkboard, the leaden windows. There was more dust on everything now, but he thought he could still make out the Latin words that the teacher had written on the chalkboard.

Inter vivos et mortuos.

Yes, this most definitely was the place.

He turned to Michael.

"I need you to take the two detectives and put them in the corner. I want them to see this, to *know* what happened here today."

Michael nodded and shoved the older detective roughly in the back. Then Carson started to move the desks to the sides of the room. Bella joined in, and in only a few minutes they had cleared the center. Satisfied, Carson walked to the middle and started to remove his clothes.

"What the fuck are you doing?" Ed demanded. Michael drove his fist into the man's gut, and he buckled. He reared back to punch him again, but Carson stopped him.

"That's enough, Michael."

The man frowned, but instead of punching, he shoved them both to the floor. They grunted as they landed roughly on the hard surface.

Even though Ed had been the one who had been struck, it was Hugh who was breathing in short gasps, unable to catch his breath.

After removing his clothes, Carson folded them neatly and then placed them on one of the desks. Then he went back to the center of the room and took a seat, cross-legged, hands on his thighs.

"Bella, I need you to guide me again," he said, and then closed his eyes and took a deep breath.

He waited, sensing her trepidation. With a nod of his head, he encouraged her.

It was time.

Somewhere far away, he heard Bella's voice, but he didn't concentrate on it. Instead, he focused on the dead, instructing them to enter the room, to form a circle around him.

In his mind, he saw them do his bidding, and then reach out and hold each other's hands like some sort of grotesque Ring Around the Rosie.

When their hands met, he felt a pressure start to build inside his chest.

Good, this is good.

Then he focused on Bella's voice, and went deeper than he had ever been before.

Chapter 34

"WHAT THE FUCK IS this?" Agent Brett Cherry mumbled. He reached over and grabbed his flask, tried to take a sip, but realizing that it was empty, threw it to the ground. "What the *fuck* is this?"

Blinking madly, he rubbed at his eyes. For a second, he thought he was drunk, passed out, and was imagining things. He actually pinched his arm, but the sharp pain confirmed that he was, indeed, awake.

Even though they had had a head start, Brett had caught up to the truck about ten minutes before it pulled into the orphanage parking lot. He knew it was the truck based on the weight of the vehicle, the way it was lower on the back axis, and the tracks that it made on the derelict road and driveway matched those outside the crematorium. But if he needed further proof, then all he had to wait for was the lithe lady with the stern expression and strange short haircut to hop out of the truck and open the back. It was nearly dark out, but the sliver of light the moon provided was just enough for Brett to make out what was in the truck.

"Fuck is this?" he said for what felt like the hundredth time.

Ed and his partner Hugh were pulled out of the back, their hands bound behind them. Ed slipped, pulling the both of them to the ground.

Brett swore again, and resisted bolting from his car.

He had parked far from the truck, pulling up behind a tree a quarter mile away. And now he was looking at his old friend through a pair of small binoculars. He pulled them away from his face when Ed landed hard in the mud, and turned his eyes skyward. He wished he had some night vision goggles, because in under an hour, the orphanage will be bathed in darkness.

But he hadn't thought this far ahead. In fact, he hadn't thought he would be on the road at all today.

Brett put the lenses back to his face and continued watching. The woman took the two detectives around the front of the truck, and then the doors opened. Brett recognized the first as Michael Young, followed by a thin man that he had never seen before. As they started toward the entrance of Sacred Heart, he almost followed them with his eyes. But something in his periphery, motion from the back of the truck, caused him to stop short.

There were more people in there.

But they weren't *people*, not really.

The bodies were moving strangely, all angular, twitchy, and they literally fell out of the truck. Squinting hard, Brett could see that they were all pale, bordering on gray, with clothes that were either torn or nonexistent.

And that said nothing of their faces, their completely black eyes, the dark blue veins that covered their heads and bodies like roads on a map.

Their stitches, their bruises.

He suddenly felt sick, remembering Kendra in the swamp.

His first thought—hope, really—was that they would lie in the mud where they fell, and he could chalk it all up to an alcoholic mirage.

But that wasn't the case. One by one they rose, pulling themselves from the mud, not bothering to wipe away the thick clumps. And then they wordlessly stumbled after the others.

For a full minute after the truck had finally been abandoned, Brett just sat and watched. And then he reached for his flask again, before remembering that it was still empty.

"Fuck this shit," he said, as he pulled his car door open. "Fuck all of this shit."

And then he headed after them, pushing Director Ames's words from his mind.

Chapter 35

"IT'S HAPPENING," ROBERT WHISPERED. "Jesus, it's happening...we need to hurry."

He could feel a tension in his chest, as if his ribs were suddenly too small for his body. He looked over at Cal, and was surprised to see that the man was staring at him, a queer expression on his face. For an instant, he felt bad for his old friend, as the man clearly felt left out of this whole ordeal, particularly since it had come to light that Shelly was also a Guardian.

A quick glance at Sean and the Cloak in the front seat and he knew that they felt the pressure, too.

Something was happening.

Carson was meddling again, trying to open the rift.

Sean let out a gasp and grasped at his heart.

"Carson is there, too. Shelly...Carson, they're both at Sacred Heart."

The Cloak muttered something under his breath.

"Why—ahh, fuck," Robert keeled over, grunting and wheezing at the pain.

Cal reached over and laid a hand on his back.

"Robbo, you alright?"

With great effort, he managed to straighten himself out and pull in a full breath.

"Fine," he croaked. "Why...why is Carson there?"

"He knows...he knows what happened there. He thinks he can use the dead to help him."

Robert squinted hard.

"I though the prophecy said that only a Guardian—"

"There were Guardians there once, nineteen of them. But..."

The Cloak's voice broke, leaving him unable to continue.

"What do you mean? What happened—?"

Cal suddenly piped up.

"Are we seriously doing this *again*?"

"Doing what?" Robert asked, gritting his teeth against the pain. All of the pressure had caused his finger to burst open, and he tried desperately to apply new gauze without drawing too much attention.

"*This*. Barging into a fucking hell house full of ghosts without a plan."

It seemed ridiculous, even to Robert, who was still confused about the role that Sacred Heart Orphanage played in all of this. The only thing that his research had revealed was that it used to be one of the largest orphanages in the northeast, but had been abandoned more than fifty years ago. Two decades later, a rich developer had tried to buy the place and turn it into condos, but a white knight, an undisclosed buyer, had swooped in and scooped it up before the deal was finalized. Based on everything he had read, nothing had been done with the place since.

A plan *would* have been nice, but there was no time. They needed to hurry before Carson—

"I have a plan," Aiden offered from the back. It was the first time in a long while that the man had spoken, and he drew the attention of everyone in the car. "I'll stand point with Ol' Betsy, make sure that no one leaves the orphanage. Robert, you—"

"Wait, how do we even know the gun will work? I mean, have you tried using it since...since...?"

Aiden nodded.

"It'll work."

Yet despite the man's confidence, Robert wasn't so sure.

"Sean and Robert, you guys take the lead. Find out where Carson and Shelly are inside the orphanage. The goal is to draw

Carson out, get Shelly to safety. Cloak and Cal, you go in next. Support for Sean and Robert. Remember, if you find any ghosts, stay clear."

If?

Robert thought that it was a fairly weak plan, especially coming from Aiden. Cal evidently felt the same.

"That's your plan? What the hell are we supposed to do when Robert and Sean find Carson? And what about Carson's cannibal friend? His psycho girlfriend?"

Aiden's eyes narrowed at the mention of Carson's girlfriend.

"Dealing with Carson and his crew is your job. I'll take care of the ghosts."

Cal went silent, as he was clearly recalling the horrors back at the Estate, at Seaforth.

"This is it," Robert said more to himself than anyone else. "It ends here."

For the next five minutes, they drove in silence. Even when the orphanage loomed into view, no one said anything.

There were clouds above the large, drab building, menacing gray clouds that seemed to be spinning in a circle directly over top of it. There was a flicker of light embedded deep inside the brewing storm, and Robert was instantly reminded of the fire in the Marrow, the crack of lightning that preceded Leland's arrival.

He shook his head, trying to stay focused. He didn't know if he came across Carson—*when* he came across Carson—if he would be able to do what he couldn't back at Seaforth.

But he had no choice.

Shelly was involved now, as was his unborn child.

You have to, Robert, Helen thought in his head. *You have to end this once and for all. You have to protect yours, protect this Earth, and you have to send me home.*

***

Sean parked the car beside the white truck, and they got out in pairs, just as Aiden had instructed. Only the man himself waited by the car, readying his gun.

The sky above them had since erupted into a storm, and the wind picked up to such a level that Robert had to huddle inward to avoid being swept up by the whirling dervish. He stayed close to Sean as they ran toward the building. In minutes, they had passed ahead of Cal and the Cloak, leaving them behind to become the second wave of attack.

Robert prepped Helen, fearing that he might have to let her take over again, and soon.

She was ready.

As he approached the massive front doors that had been wedged open, memories started flooding back to him, much like they had when he had stepped into Callahan's church. Memories of a time here, in this gray orphanage.

Does anyone know what the words Inter vivos et mortuos *means?* he remembered the teacher asking.

Robert pressed his palm flat against the door and leaned against it, trying to alleviate the pressure in his chest.

But he couldn't; it only seemed to grow.

As soon as his hand made contact, something flashed in his mind—an image of Carson, seated on the ground, a cloud opening above his head.

Robert turned to Sean, suddenly finding it difficult to breathe.

"We have to hurry."

The man nodded, and Robert could see in his face that he too felt the pressure. Sean grabbed the door and carefully opened it.

A gray light surrounded them, as if the place itself radiated some sort of ambient glow.

Robert had taken less than a handful of steps inside Sacred Heart when he saw the first of the dead.

Chapter 36

ED BLINKED HARD, THINKING that maybe after Michael had bitten off part of Hugh's ear, he had stridden over and killed him.

Ate him, too, maybe, but Ed hoped that that happened after he was already dead.

There was just no other explanation for what he was witnessing.

The bodies in the truck, *they* had been dead. There was no questioning that. After all, he had stopped Vinny thirty miles from the crematorium and had seen them then. He had even fucking laid in the back of the truck with their stinking corpses.

But now they weren't.

Now they were standing, teetering, holding hands in a giant fucking kumbaya circle like a demented séance.

And in the middle was a man who was worse...far worse than even Michael. Michael, who trapped women in his basement, who nibbled on their skin, their bones, their sinew while they were still alive.

This man held power over the dead, however bizarre the thought sounded in his head, and if Ed was to believe this, then he also had to believe that he was going to commandeer even more of them.

A sudden blast of wind hit him in the face, and his eyes immediately glanced upward. The ceiling had either torn away, despite the fact that no debris had fallen inward, or had simply become transparent by some strange trick or magic.

Whatever the case, the clouds high above were dark, foreboding, and lightning illuminated their rounded edges as they swirled.

"Come to me, rise up and come to me...enter me," Carson whispered, his words pulled from his mouth and whipped upward into the storm above. The chairs and tables at the periphery of the room started shaking, and even though he was reluctant to take his eyes away from Carson, Ed felt the need to check on Hugh, who hadn't said anything since their time in the back of the truck.

"Hugh, what—?"

But Michael elbowed him hard in the ribs, and he winced, bending to that side.

Hugh looked over at him, his eyes big as saucers. He was nearly as pale as the dead making a circle not more than ten feet from them.

Whatever was happening, whatever fucking demons that Carson was conjuring from the depths of hell, Ed was certain of one thing: he didn't want to be here when they arrived.

But with his hands bound, and strapped to Hugh and with Michael watching on, he had no idea how he was going to free the both of them.

Bella was walking around the circle, whispering something to Carson, who was still nude, eyes closed, in the center of the dead.

He thought that perhaps he might be able to overtake her, given her level of distraction, although he hadn't forgotten how quickly she had gotten the drop on him when they had hopped out of the back of the truck.

More lightning split the sky, and Ed instinctively tucked his head into his shoulders.

He noticed that Michael did the same.

There was a table not too far from him, just on the other side of Hugh.

If I could somehow manage to—

More lightning filled the room, but this time, it didn't seem to come from the sky above, but from Carson himself.

The dead stopped walking in a circle, and stepped back, their hands and heads falling to their sides, offering Ed a clear view of the nude man.

"Jesus," he whispered, unable to control himself. But Michael didn't deliver another blow to his side as he expected; instead, he heard the man sharply inhale.

Thin, smoking streams of light were spilling from Carson's eyes and mouth and his chin shot upward. And then the room was suddenly filled with an intense, blinding brightness, so vivid that Ed was forced to close his eyes.

If his hands had been free, he would have used them to shield his face.

In the blinding light, he heard Carson's voice loud and clear, and a shudder ran up his spine.

"They're here...they've arrived."

Chapter 37

CAL WATCHED HIS FRIEND and Sean head toward the orphanage and crouched down low. As per the plan, he waited, even though every single muscle in his entire body screamed at him to move.

To run.

To run as far away from Sacred Heart Orphanage as his fucking legs would take him.

The Cloak crouched beside him, his old spine stooped, the dark black fabric turning his body into what looked like a pile of refuse.

"How long do we wait, Aiden?" he asked.

When there was no reply, he looked over his shoulder.

The dead man was gone.

"Great."

"We wait until they reach the door," the Cloak croaked. "And then we go around back."

Cal observed the man for a moment, trying to figure out what the hell he was all about. Small in stature, definitely old. The hood of the cloak covered the top part of his face, his hair, his eyes, while the turtleneck hid the lower half. Cal had no idea how the man even saw. Then he remembered the camera around his neck and started to raise it, intending on pointing it at the Cloak. But before he did, the Cloak spoke again and his hand held in midair.

"You're a good friend, Cal."

Cal made a face, the man's assessment of him coming as a surprise.

"How do you know?" he retorted. "How the hell would you know?"

The Cloak turned his head back toward the house.

"They're at the door. Let's go."

He started to rise, but Cal reached out and grabbed his arm.

"Wait—"

The Cloak shook him off.

"It's time. We need to hurry."

Chapter 38

CARSON MUST HAVE KNOWN that they were coming, as he had seven corpses standing just inside the doorway, and as soon as Robert and Sean crossed the threshold, they lunged at them.

"Fuck!" Robert shouted, twisting as a man with huge black lips slipped by him. The next one came at Sean, and a split second before he moved, Robert heard a hissing noise like boiling air in his bloodied ear.

The bullet passed right through the skull of the man with the thick lips, and then struck the quiddity coming at Sean in the center of his chest behind him.

"Jesus Christ!" Robert shouted. He whipped his head around to see where the shot had come from, but the sky was so dark outside that he saw nothing.

But he knew it was Aiden, and when he turned back, he knew that what the man had said was true.

The gun *would* work.

The first quiddity fell flat on his face without even bracing himself and went still. Robert was about to look away when the quiddity suddenly started to shake, tiny tremors at first, but these quickly devolved into a massive grand mal seizure.

At the height of these violent muscle contractions, the man's back arched and his pitch-black eyes stared directly into Robert.

Then he went still again and dissolved into a cloud of black dirt and dust.

Robert instinctively brought the crook of his elbow to his mouth to avoid inhaling the cloud of quiddity. But his actions were unnecessary; the cloud shot upward, seemingly passing directly through the ceiling above.

He looked over at Sean, who was staring at the other quiddity as it too fell to his knees and then started to shake.

A blur of motion caught his eye, and Robert's face shot up.

"Sean! Another one—*look out!*"

There was another whizzing sound, and this quiddity was also gunned down by Aiden.

We need to get out of here, there are too many, Helen chimed in his head. *Robert, something bad is happening here...*

No shit.

Another shot rang out, and another corpse collapsed.

And yet they kept coming. Robert had initially counted eight, but it seemed as if there were dozens of them now, maybe even hundreds clambering over each to get to them. To get their hands on the living.

He blinked hard, trying to stay focused.

"Go back outside," Sean yelled at him over the roar of the storm that suddenly sounded as if it were originating from *inside* the orphanage instead of outside. "Get the fuck outside so Aiden can take them out."

Robert nodded and was about to take a step backward when he saw something partway down the hallway.

A familiar silhouette.

A familiar *pregnant* silhouette.

"*Shelly!*" he shouted over the sound of the seizing quiddity and the wind whipping about his ears. "Shelly!"

But she didn't turn.

And then the entire orphanage went white a second before one of the quiddity lunged at him.

Robert did the only thing he knew how, in that moment. The only thing that would keep him from being sent to the Marrow.

He let Helen take over.

Chapter 39

CAL WAS WORKING HIS away around the side of the building when he heard Robert's shout.

"Shelly! *Shelly!*"

He immediately froze, ignoring the Cloak's pleas to come with him, to hurry.

Shelly, the one who he had brought into the fold, was in danger. Shelly, the one that Robert had impregnated, was inside the orphanage. Shelly, the one who was pregnant with the baby that had the potential to hold the rift in the Marrow open, was within Carson's reach.

Cal swiveled on his heels, turning back toward the front of the building.

"Cal," the Cloak hissed after him. "Cal, come back!"

But Cal didn't listen. He was nearly at the front entrance when the entire orphanage erupted into a ball of light.

Chapter 40

"YOU FEEL THAT?" BEN asked Allan, looking over at him.

The sky had gotten progressively darker in the Marrow until it had become nearly completely black. The sand, previously velvety smooth on the soles of his bare feet, was suddenly getting hot and sticky.

"I feel it," Allan admitted. "It's getting stronger...*he's* coming."

Ben, who had been staring up at the clouds that had started to turn a deep orange, looked at Allan. The boy was scared, terrified even.

"Who? Who's coming?"

Allan swallowed hard, his Adam's apple bobbing violently in his narrow throat.

"The Goat. The Goat is coming."

Ben shivered just as the sky erupted into flames.

Chapter 41

AGENT BRETT CHERRY TOOK a wide berth around the two vehicles as he made his way to the rear of the orphanage. He had his pistol drawn, but something inside him told him that it would do little good.

His time in the swamp had taught him as much.

Fire, on the other hand...

Lightning cracked in the sky above, and Brett looked upward. The storm clouds appeared to be circling, twisting and turning in on themselves, forming some sort of spire that ascended from the peaked roof of the orphanage to the heavens above.

In the center of that spire, he could pick out the unmistakable sight of flames.

A fire in the sky.

Brett took a deep breath, picked up the pace, and headed towards that very spire.

"This is for you, Ken-Ken. For you."

Chapter 42

THE BRIGHT LIGHT STILL blinded him, and when a hand slipped around his neck and pulled him close, he almost called out.

But the hand over his mouth prevented him from doing so.

Hot breath was suddenly on his ear.

"Don't move."

Ed's chest deflated. It was Brett. The man must have snuck into the room under the cover of the storm and the light.

He felt pressure on his arms, then the sudden release as his hands were cut free. Ed immediately alternated rubbing his wrists, trying to work some feeling back into his fists.

"Come with me," Brett whispered, his breath reeking of alcohol. "Follow me exactly and I can get us out of here."

Ed slowly made his way to his feet as silently as possible, remembering that Michael was very close.

As was Hugh.

Recalling the man's saucer eyes, the pale face, his slack jaw, he doubted that Hugh even realized that he was no longer bound to Ed.

"Wait," he whispered. "We can't leave Hugh."

Then the light blinked out.

Ed and Brett froze.

"They're here," Carson whispered again.

The storm had died too, and the room was suddenly very quiet—*too* quiet.

And then Bella switched on a lamp, and Ed's heart stopped.

Carson was still in the circle now, only he wasn't the only one surrounded by the quiddity that had rode with him in the back of the truck.

There were others. And these others were hugging him, holding him, clinging to his legs.

There were seven of them, six boys and one girl ranging in age from what Ed guessed was five to eleven.

His heart suddenly started again, and for whatever reason, this gave him away. All of the children turned to look at Ed with their obsidian pits for eyes.

"I've brought the Guardians back," Carson said with a smile. "I've brought them all back."

He patted one boy on the head, then turned around and focused on Brett.

"You're Agent Cherry, I assume?" Carson asked.

Brett tried to bolt, but Michael stood in his path, blocking his way. Brett raised his gun and aimed it at the man's forehead.

"I don't understand fuck all of what's going on here, and I could care two shits about it. But I'll tell you one thing: me and my friends are leaving here right fucking now."

Carson smiled, and Ed thought that his mouth had gotten bigger, more full of teeth. And they seemed to have been filed into points.

"No, I don't think so."

Carson flicked his chin, and the quiddity that had been encircling him suddenly started to move toward Ed and Brett. Their gait was still awkward, but had improved compared to when he had first seen them fall out of the back of the truck.

Brett immediately swung the gun from Michael to the quiddity closest to them.

"Stop," he instructed. "Stop moving."

This wasn't a prolonged standoff. When the quiddity didn't stop, Brett squeezed off one round.

The bullet struck a male corpse in the shoulder, but aside from twisting to that side from the impact, it didn't even slow him.

"Brett, I don't—"

But Ed didn't finish his sentence before Brett fired off two more shots in rapid succession. This time, the bullets hit the man in the head.

The result, however, was the same.

"Fuck!" Brett shouted. He took a step forward, held the gun directly out in front of him at arm's length.

Somewhere in front of them, Carson burst into laughter.

The window to their left suddenly exploded and a high-pressure round hit the man that Brett had been shooting directly in the temple. Brett made a confused face, and stared at his gun, as the man's head was completely vaporized.

It fell to its knees, and then started to shake.

Carson stopped laughing.

"Bella! Get down!" he cried.

Another shot exploded the second window in the classroom, and another quiddity was felled.

Carson roared in anger.

A third shot, a third smashed window. This time, however, the bullet struck Bella directly in the back as she dove to the floor.

But nothing happened.

Ed watched, his confused expression matching hers as she patted herself, looking for a wound that simply didn't exist.

Brett, finally overcoming the shock that gripped him, whipped the gun around to Michael again. But the man had moved, and before Ed could warn his friend, Michael drove his fist into the side of Brett's head. Agent Cherry staggered, stumbling dangerously close to the remaining quiddity.

Ed pounced, but he wasn't in as good a shape as he had once been. It was an awkward lunge, reminiscent of the quiddity stumbling out of the truck. Michael sidestepped and then delivered two punches to Ed's side and stomach, immediately winding him.

He crumpled into a ball, gasping for air.

"Hugh," he tried to say, but only air came out of his mouth. "Hugh, help me."

Michael came out of nowhere, delivering another blow, this time to his chin. Ed's head snapped back, and he felt his teeth gnash together, covering his tongue in sawdust.

Ed fell on his ass, then collapsed against the back wall. He fought against creeping unconsciousness, knowing that if he succumbed to the darkness, he would never waken.

The teetering quiddity would get to him.

As he blinked, trying to clear his vision, he realized that there was someone hovering over him.

It was Michael, and like Carson somewhere behind him, he was smiling.

"I'm going to enjoy eating you."

But then something flew into his side, driving him to the floor. Ed scrambled to his feet, watching as Brett rained down fists on Michael like a man possessed. A snarl from his left drew his attention, and he realized that one of the dead was inches from Hugh, who appeared frozen in place.

"No!" he shouted, grabbing his partner by the shoulders and spinning him away. As he pulled him, something whizzed by his ear and the quiddity's left arm exploded. Like the others, he fell to the ground and started to seize.

Ed looked to his partner.

"Hugh, snap the fuck out of it!" he ordered. "Get your shit together, we have to get the fuck out of here, now!"

Hugh's eyes went wide and he raised his hand to point, but before he could even bring it to shoulder level, Ed felt something cold and sharp slide into his body just above his hip. It was so clean, so fast, that at first he didn't even feel any pain.

Looking down, however, he saw the glint of a blade, and the top of someone's head, which was covered in short black hair.

Bella had gotten to him again.

Chapter 43

"ROBERT," SEAN GASPED FROM his left. "What have you done?"

But Robert hadn't done anything.

When the light blinked out, and the ambient glow returned, Robert realized that he was gripping a corpse by the throat.

Or, more specifically, *Helen* was gripping him.

And yet, Robert could feel the texture of his waxy skin beneath his fingers, and he could smell his foul, rotting breath on his face.

He expected to be taken to the Marrow, to see Amy again, and part of him wanted that. Then he remembered Shelly.

She's here and she needs my help.

Helen responded by squeezing even harder, picking the dead man right off the floor. Robert had never experienced this much strength, this much power in his entire life, not even the last time Helen had taken over and together they had grabbed Carson.

"Robert."

Helen pulled hard, and the man's throat tore away like overcooked turkey. Then she shoved him backward, as he lay on the ground gasping. A second later, he started to twitch, not unlike the quiddity that Aiden had blasted.

They came at him all at once then, the remaining four quiddity, all with hands outstretched, desperate to tear at his living flesh. Out of the corner of his eye, he saw Sean back away.

"Go!" Robert shouted. "Go and save Shelly! I'll take care of these! Hurry!"

Sean nodded, and then Robert balled his fist as they lunged at him all at once.

***

Sean couldn't believe what he had seen.

Robert had actually grabbed the dead, and he was still here. It went against everything that he had ever read, that had ever been taught to him, that he had ever *seen*.

If the quiddity touched a living soul, then they would be transported to the Marrow together. It was paramount, it was idiosyncratic to the separation, the idea that the two worlds were never supposed to mix, that they could *never* mix.

But Robert had done just that.

Sean hurried down the hallway, his legs moving of their own accord. Confusion overwhelmed him, but he tried his best to compartmentalize these feelings.

He still had a job to do.

Squinting in the dim light, he chased toward the last spot that he had seen Shelly.

As he did, a moment of clarity suddenly struck him.

If Robert could touch them and not get sent to the Marrow, then that could only mean one thing.

Robert was already dead.

Chapter 44

SHELLY HAD BEEN HERE before. She knew that now, for a fact. She had been in Sacred Heart Orphanage when she was younger.

When something horrible had happened, when all of them had been murdered.

All but three of them.

She stumbled down the hallway, confused as to why she had come back here, her mind a mess ever since she had found the photograph of her in the church.

The one that Robert had left for her.

Her fingertips brushed against the wall as she walked, feeling the hardness of the brick, the thin layer of dust like a covering of her soul.

Robert...

She loved him, she finally realized, even though she thought that she had felt this way for some time now.

But she wasn't sure that the feeling was mutual. There was something about him, a huge hunk of him that still clung to the past. She saw it in his face, in his eyes, in his very quiddity.

Knew it like she knew the baby inside her was a baby girl.

He hadn't let go of Amy yet, and she wasn't even sure that he had let go of Wendy, either.

She swallowed hard, and then felt that crushing pain in her chest again. Only now it was deeper, lower, in her guts, in her stomach. In her womb.

Shelly kept on moving, her feet barely rising off the floor now, just dusty, shuffling steps.

Her mind flashed back to that time, to the others running out of the classroom, while for some reason she had been compelled to run back in. And that was when Sean had found her.

And had brought her to the boiler room.

Which was where she was headed now, guided by long-lost memories of decades ago, like some sort of organic GPS.

Only Shelly had no idea what the arrow pointed at, where her final destination was.

Or what was waiting for her when she got there.

Chapter 45

CAL'S JAW DROPPED WHEN he saw Robert, his fists covered in gore, the quiddity all around him.

"No! No, no, no!" he shouted.

Either Robert didn't hear him, or was already on his way to the Marrow; he didn't turn. Instead, he kept raining down punches, and tearing—there was a horrible tearing sound in the hallway—as chunks of dead flesh were tossed around.

Cal jumped to one side to avoid a hunk of hair or scalp. As he did, the camera around his neck smacked him in the chest, reminding him that it was still there.

He raised it up to his eyes, and looked through the view-finder.

What he saw took his breath away. Nearly the entire field of vision was filled with bright light of the quiddity. Every piece of shrapnel was glowing, peppering the field of view. But that wasn't what made him gasp.

That was Robert himself. Instead of being dim, gray, like the man at the cemetery had been, Robert was so bright that it was difficult for Cal to look directly at him.

Robert growled and tossed more rotting flesh to the ground, as Cal pressed the trigger. At first, nothing happened. Then, the remaining thrashing quiddity started to slow, their movements becoming more labored. As did Robert's.

The man turned to him then.

"Cal, stop...the camera," he gasped. His voice was strange, as if it weren't completely his. Like it someone else speaking through his mouth and lips.

Cal was torn, not sure what to do next. He kept his finger on the button.

***

Something's happening to me, Helen thought. *Something's happening, I'm being...I'm being pulled.*

Robert felt it too, although he was for some reason convinced that it was only affecting Helen and not him.

His head turned, and that was when he realized that Cal had entered the orphanage and was aiming the camera directly at him.

"Turn it off," he tried to say, but with Helen in control of him, the words came out strange, almost garbled. "Cal, turn off the camera."

His friend had a confused expression on his face, and when it was clear that he wasn't going to listen, Robert felt the urge to come to the fore again.

But he had to wait—wait for the rest of the dying and dead to be gone. He didn't, couldn't, be in control when he was still in contact with him.

Please, Robert, you need to take over, I'm being pulled and I don't think—

Several of the corpses that Helen had decimated turned to vapor, while others still, the ones that she hadn't torn apart yet, started to slow, to be locked in place by the camera.

It would only be a minute or so before he was in the same boat, and he wasn't sure if that happened if he would ever be able to take ownership of his own body ever again.

Not yet, Helen, not yet.

He felt Helen try to move, try to speak, but she couldn't manage. She was still in charge, in control, but she was also frozen.

Robert managed to look around, and saw that there was just one more quiddity, a woman in a torn wedding dress reaching for him. Her fingers were outstretched, the nails horribly long and yellow from where the cuticle had peeled back in death.

Not yet, not yet, not yet…

He could feel Helen try to get away, to move back from the woman, but Robert's body didn't behave. Then the hand stopped, mere inches from his left eye, and Robert could wait no longer.

He burst forward, upward, as if desperately trying to break the surface of a body of water. At first, he just bounced back, as if the water had been covered in ice. He tried again, desperately trying to put himself back behind his eyes, in his head, in control.

For the briefest of moments, he thought that it wouldn't be possible, that the camera had frozen the water, and that he would be trapped as an observer forever in his own body.

But then he broke through.

Robert stumbled forward, spinning just in time to avoid the woman's outstretched claw.

"Robert!" Cal shouted.

Robert stepped over the remaining pieces of dead bodies, those that hadn't vaporized yet, and then turned to his friend.

"What the fuck happened? What was happening to you? How did you…?" Cal rambled, the camera still held up in front of him.

Robert shook his head.

Helen? You still here?

No response.

Guilt swept over him then. Had he waited too long? He had promised the woman that he would take her to the Marrow, give her the choice like everyone else.

But not like this, not banished like—

I'm here.

Robert let out a sigh of relief.

"It wasn't me, Cal. It was Helen—she took over. And she's already dead, the quiddity can't take her."

Cal's eyebrows knitted in confusion, but Robert also saw some semblance of understanding cross his features.

"I need to go!" Robert shouted hurrying down the hallway. "I need to find Shelly!"

"Wait! What about me! What about the fucking quiddity?"

Robert didn't look back as he broke into a sprint.

"Stay there! Keep them at bay!"

Chapter 46

ED COLLAPSED ON THE ground, breathing heavily. His hands were covered in blood from the knife that Bella had stuck him with. Looking into her dark eyes, he knew that she wanted to keep sticking him, plugging him full of holes. But Carson had shouted to her, told her to go get Shelly, whoever the fuck that was.

And then they were surrounded again. Michael had gotten the best of Agent Cherry, and his friend was slumped beside him. Hugh was also seated, although he was still staring blankly into space, his face slack.

And the dead were all around them.

It was only a matter of time before they lunged at them again.

And when that happened, there would be nothing they could do about it.

He took a deep breath, and accepted the fact that he was going to die. Staring at Carson's smiling face, the bowed heads of the dead children still huddled against him, Ed began to reconsider whether or not everyone had good in them.

This man, this demon conjurer, was pure evil.

Chapter 47

SEAN KNEW WHERE SHELLY was going, even before he saw her outline up ahead. His first instinct was to call after her, to hurry and catch her, but something held him back.

It was the thought he had had while he'd been bound by Robert and his ragtag team of ghostbusters.

Shelly and her baby were what Carson needed to keep the rift open.

He pressed himself against the wall when Shelly hesitated, her head turning slightly.

She didn't see him.

A moment later, she broke into a sprint, moving as quickly as her large body would allow, and Sean followed. Another figure appeared from a room on his left, and Sean fell even further behind.

Even though he had never met the woman, he knew who she was based on the descriptions provided by both Robert and Aiden.

The woman with the short black hair moved like some sort of cat, sliding and gliding across the floor with unprecedented dexterity. Sean reached for his pistol on his hip, but then realized that Robert had taken that away from him long ago, and he hadn't thought about asking for it back.

He doubted that the man would have given it to him anyway.

Shelly took a sharp turn to the right, and the woman followed, not making a sound. There was no way that Shelly knew she was being followed by Bella. And yet Sean still didn't call out, didn't even move to warn her.

Even when Shelly went into the small boiler room and Bella followed, he just sat in wait.

He propped himself against the other side of the door and listened.

"You," Shelly said with such disdain that Sean thought that her voice carried had an actual weight to it. "What the fuck do you want?"

"Carson says you need to come with me. He wants to have a chat."

"Fuck him, I'm not going anywhere."

There was a pause. The door had no window, but even if there were one, Sean wouldn't have risked looking in. Instead, he bowed his head and continued to listen, his mind already made up.

Shelly and her child were just too dangerous.

"What are you going to do with that? Stab me? Cut my baby out? I will claw your fucking eyes out, bitch."

Bella laughed.

"Carson wants to see you, Shelly. It's in your best interest to come with me before I have to use this."

Shelly growled.

"You wouldn't do that to a pregnant…"

"Sean, what are you doing?" a gruff voice whispered from his left. Sean whipped around, hands at the ready.

He straightened his posture when he saw a cloaked figure approach.

"I asked you what you were doing," the Cloak demanded, taking an aggressive step forward. "Is that Bella in there, with Shelly? Why aren't you going to her?"

Sean subconsciously moved in front of the door, blocking his path.

"I—I can't," he said at last. "I need to protect the integrity of the Marrow, and every minute that the child is allowed to grow, every second it gets closer to birth, the more danger we're all in."

The Cloak froze.

"What—what are you saying? Sean, what are you saying?"

Sean lowered his head.

"I'm saying that she can't—fuck, the baby can't make it to term."

For several seconds, the only sound that Sean heard was the two women arguing inside the boiler room.

"Get out of my way," the Cloak demanded at last.

Sean shook his head.

"I can't do that. I am a Guardian, and it is my duty to keep the Marrow safe. I'm sorry, I just can't let you go in there."

A sound came from the Cloak then, something that made Sean's eyes water, and the hair on the back of his neck stand at attention.

It took him a while to realize that the Cloak was laughing.

"You won't let me? *ME?!* I gave you your power and I can take it away!" he growled.

The bickering in the room behind Sean suddenly stopped and his heart started beating loudly in his chest.

This wasn't how he had seen things going. Still, the Cloak was old, withered, and his time had come to an end. This was the only rational choice, even if his elder didn't see it that way.

The Cloak took a step forward, a shuffle, and Sean readied himself.

He hadn't wanted it to come to this.

But there was no other option.

The gates to the Marrow could never be opened.

"I gave you your power," the Cloak repeated as he reached up and grabbed the lip of the black hood. "And I can take it away."

In one smooth motion, the Cloak pulled the hood back, while at the same time yanking down the turtleneck.

"No," Sean moaned, stumbling backward. His back slammed into the door. "No, it can't be, please, no, no, no…"

Someone hammered on the door behind him, trying to get out, but he took no notice.

And in that moment, Sean realized why the Cloak hadn't gotten upset at the report that Carson was dead—it was because he had been still alive.

A mother just knew.

"Please," he sobbed.

Chapter 48

As soon as Robert turned the corner, he was thrown into a reverie like a lobster into boiling water.

His eyes rolled back and his heels skidded on the dust-covered floor as his body came to an almost cartoonish stop.

He was at his desk sitting beside his brother, staring at the stern-faced teacher in front of him. She was pretty, but strict. Fair, but deliberate.

"Who knows what this says?" she asked, pointing to the Latin words on the chalkboard.

Of course Robert knew what they were, but he didn't raise his hand right away. He didn't want to look like the teacher's pet, like he was getting special treatment. He looked over at his brother, but the boy didn't seem to be paying attention.

Typical.

"Anyone?"

Eventually, Robert raised his hand, and his mother immediately pointed at him.

"Robert?"

"It says *Inter vivos et mortuos,* and it means the land between the living and the dead."

Robert returned to the present with a stumble, barely stopping himself before he fell flat on his face.

Something bad had happened here, something horrible.

Something horrible had happened to his friends, to his mother.

But he couldn't deal with that now, couldn't even think about it. Right now, he had to find Shelly.

His mind took him to the room near the back of the orphanage.

The one that he used to have lessons in long ago.

Without thinking, he burst through the door to the room, then immediately stopped short.

"Ah, my dear brother. I expected you to show, but so soon? Always the more eager student, isn't that right?"

Robert's eyes narrowed as he surveyed the scene before him.

Carson was in the center of the room, naked, and he was surrounded by what looked like a harem of young boys. Near the back of the class, he caught sight of Michael, and more of the quiddity like the ones at the front door. The corpses were surrounding three people that he didn't recognize, all of whom looked injured. All of whom were alive.

"Let them go," Robert demanded, taking another step forward.

"Who?" Carson asked, smiling. The boys and one girl that surrounded him all hung their heads low, but Robert felt that there was something familiar about them nonetheless.

"The men at the back of the room. Let them go."

Carson laughed.

"Them? Who are they? A bunch of cops that don't know anything. Who cares about them? I thought you would want me to release—"

Robert's eyes narrowed.

Shelly.

But when Carson raised his hand and the kids looked up, Robert realized that he wasn't talking about Shelly at all.

"—your old friends. *Our* old friends."

No, he was talking about the boys and the one girl.

Tears immediately welled in Robert's eyes as he recognized some of their faces, and he was taken back to his childhood again.

He was in a tunnel of sorts, some sort of aluminum tube, looking down through a grate. The kids were there, as well as the teacher, his mother, and they were running. But there was someone else there, too, someone in a faded jean jacket and black hat.

One by one, he cut them down with a blade, slicing their soft little throats, spearing them in their thin bellies. But what he did to the woman was the worst. He took his time with her, cutting hunks of flesh off her face as she screamed for the boys and girls that were lying in puddles of their own blood.

Robert was brought back to the present by Carson's droning laughter.

"You really didn't remember, did you?"

Robert wiped the tears from his face.

"Let them go," he sobbed, but his voice lacked the authority of a few minutes ago. Deep down, he could feel Helen starting to rise, wanting to come to the fore again, to exact her vengeance on Carson, who had given him so much pain.

He pushed back.

Carson shook his head in disbelief.

"You know, I had my doubts that Leland could enact this whole plan, I seriously did. I mean, to make you forget…to bring you and Shelly together. Genius, really. And to manipulate that bastard Sean, that was classic."

Robert felt his heart pounding away in his chest.

"Wh—what?" he stammered.

Carson laughed again.

"You still don't get it, do you?"

Robert felt his head start to spin as he considered the implications of what Carson was saying.

Leland was behind all of this? Behind *everything*?

"Yes, Robert. Everything. He even caused the accident, sent one of his bumbling quiddity in front of Wendy's car that night during the storm. The lightning storm."

Robert felt so dizzy that he dropped to one knee.

"Yes, Robert. And Amy. You see, Leland had been following you for some time. He knew about Wendy and her affair, he knew that it wouldn't be enough to just take Wendy—he needed to take Amy from you, too."

"No," Robert moaned. "It's not true."

"Oh, it's true, Robert. And if you don't believe me, just hang around for another few minutes, and you can ask him yourself."

Chapter 49

"BUT...BUT I SAW you *die*," Sean whispered. "Robert saw you die."

"I didn't die," Chloe Black croaked. "He tried to kill me, but he didn't."

Sean swallowed hard and stared at her face. It was horrible; she was bald, and her scalp was viciously gnarled, like the rolls on the back of a fat man's neck.

But her face was worse. She had no nose, just a hole in the center, and her left eye was missing. From her cheeks down, the skin was flayed; in some spots, it hadn't healed completely, even after all these years. She had no lips; her mouth was but a slit just above her chin.

And the mutilation didn't stop there. There was a long vertical gash running across her throat, which explained why her voice was so horribly disfigured.

"But those kids...I could only save a few of them, bring a few them *inside*." Her one good eye drifted upward.

Sean shook his head as he remembered the carnage looking down through the gate in the vent. There was no way that the boys could have survived; in fact, it was only by some miracle that Chloe was still here.

All this time, he'd had no idea.

And yet, it didn't change anything. Didn't change the facts. Didn't change the danger.

"If that baby in there is born..." He let his sentence trail off for a moment, before shaking his head. "We can't allow it to be born."

"Sean," Chloe rasped. "Don't make me do this."

Sean stood up straight and stepped forward.

"Do what?"

"*This*," she growled. Before he could react, she extended her hands and bowed her head. And then it started.

At first, Sean didn't know what was happening. But then he started to feel a pull, deep down in the pit of his stomach. It was like the feeling he got in his chest when the quiddity were around, but this time it felt like something was coming *out* of him.

"What are you doing?" he said, but the words were drawn out, and he barely recognized his own voice.

Chloe bore down, and Sean felt a bout of dizziness come over him. He was reminded of a time long ago, many decades prior, when he had first met Chloe and learned about the Marrow. When she had first made him a Guardian.

But now she was taking it all away.

Sean took a step forward, but he was off balance and fell to one knee.

The pulling sensation rose up through the pit of his stomach and into his chest. He threw his head back and tried to scream, but the only thing that came out was a horribly dry, croaking sound.

He was on all fours now, but even crawling was beyond his abilities. His head was spinning, remembering his time first here at the orphanage, then with Callahan, dropping off the boys, and then hunting Leland down.

Sean shook his head, trying to clear it, to focus, to stand, to figure out what the fuck the scarred woman in front of him was doing.

But it was no use.

He felt something rise up into his throat, and then it felt like his soul was pulled right out of his mouth. His youth, his essence, everything that made him a Guardian, was gone, stolen by the very person who had given them to him in the first place.

Sean collapsed to the ground, reduced to a steam and heat rising off of him.

Somewhere far away, he heard Chloe speak.

"I'm sorry, Sean. I just couldn't let this happen."

He felt a brush of hot air as Chloe walked by and pulled the door to the room behind him wide. Sean, an empty shell now, somehow managed to pull himself to his feet and stagger down the hallway.

Chapter 50

ED COULD FEEL HIS strength fading, and putting pressure on the wound in his side didn't seem to be stem the flow. He could feel his blood pulsing from between his fingers.

Never in his right mind had he thought that tracking Michael Young would put him here. The man called Robert was standing in front of the dead, and he was determined to make one last stand.

But seeing what he had, seeing what Carson had done, Ed didn't know of a way that he could possibly succeed.

"What the shit?" he grumbled. Michael turned toward him in response to his curse, just as Ed got a surprising second wind. Without thinking, he reached out and grabbed the man's arm and pivoted, spinning him around. Michael had been so rapt in what was happening between Carson and Robert that he was taken by surprise.

"No!" he shouted, struggling to right himself. He was on one foot, just an inch or two from one of the dead. Ed tried to make it to his feet, to reach out and shove the man, but the pain in his side was too great and he slumped back against the wall.

Michael smiled.

"You stupid—"

But then Hugh, who had said and done nothing ever since they had arrived at Sacred Heart Orphanage, reached out with his foot and delivered a kick to Michael's left knee.

The smile fell off his face as he fell backward, crashing into a man that had burns all over one side of his body. At first, nothing happened. In fact, if anything, the dead man actually broke his fall. But then the quiddity seemed to activate upon human touch. His arms snaked around Michael's body and he started to grab on. Michael tried to shove him off, but the man's grip was doing something to him.

He started to shake, and his eyes rolled back. And then the whites disappeared, as if ink were dropped into a hole in his skull and then drifted downward, swirling around his eyes until they went completely black.

As if the events of today hadn't already been enough, Ed saw the man actually start to fade, become slightly translucent at first, before disappearing.

Ed shut his own eyes and allowed the darkness to spread over him like a warm blanket.

Chapter 51

"No!" Carson shouted. Robert glanced over the man's shoulder and saw a commotion with the detectives and the dead.

Robert wiped his tears away and spurred to action. Using the disturbance as a distraction, he moved around Carson, away from the dead children, and hurried to the back of the room.

"Stop!" Carson shouted, but Robert just kept moving. He wouldn't let any more people die.

Carson made a sound, a horrible, guttural noise, and the quiddity surrounding the detectives started to turn, to look at him with their horrible black eyes.

Helen, I hope you're ready for this.

And then Robert fell away, dropping down into the pit of his stomach, allowing the woman to take over. She had been repressed, beaten, murdered by her husband, and in a way, he supposed that her power from beyond the grave was some sort of tangible revenge.

Revenge for everyone who had wronged her.

She grabbed the first quiddity by the throat and tore it out. The second she grabbed by the arm and spun him around. Her other hand caught his chin and yanked against the turn, snapping his neck. Both collapsed quiddity started shaking, and then turned into thick black clouds like the kind that Robert had seen at the entrance to the orphanage.

The third exploded from a high-pressure rifle blast that took out nearly his entire mid-section. Robert felt his body recoil in confusion, but when the fourth quiddity bore down, Helen dispatched him as easily as the other two.

"No!" Carson roared. "What are you doing? Robert! *Robert!*"

But Robert was only a passenger now.

Two of the three detectives, a young man with blond hair and another, a little bit older with red-rimmed eyes, looked up at him, matching terrified expressions on their faces. The other was breathing heavily, blood spilling from his side.

Carson bellowed again, and now Robert pushed himself upward, displacing the exhausted Helen.

Then he spun around.

"Carson! Let the kids go! They can't harm me! They can't take me to the Marrow."

Chapter 52

CHLOE COULD FEEL SEAN inside of her, his essence filling her very being. But this wasn't the first time that she had absorbed someone's quiddity, their soul.

She had done it before in this very place, saving three of the young boys as their lives eked out of them from the wounds delivered by her husband.

By the Goat.

She pushed Sean down with the others.

And then she threw the door to the boiler room open.

"Let her go," she croaked.

Bella peeked out from behind Shelly's head, a knife to her throat. For a second, her eyes went wide, and then she grimaced at the sight of Chloe's mangled face. But she quickly regained her composure. It was clear that, after being with Carson for so long, barely anything surprised her now.

"I don't fucking think so. Carson wants her, wants her baby. Says it's important. She is coming with me."

Chloe drew in a deep, gasping breath.

"No!" Bella shouted. "I heard what you did to Sean. You so much as breathe and I'll drive this blade deep into her soft neck. And then I'll cut the little fucking fetus out of her."

To prove that she was serious, she dug the knife into Shelly's throat, making a dimple in her skin.

Shelly gasped and tried to move, but Bella's grip held fast.

"Don't fucking move."

Chloe was frozen. If she'd had a proper brow, it would have knitted; if she'd still had tear ducts, tears would have spilled forth.

But she had neither.

"Back up. Back the fuck up."

Chloe had no choice but to obey, stepping out of the room.

It didn't make sense that she had overtaken a Guardian, one of the few Guardians remaining, and reduced him to the withering old man that he was, and yet this woman, this small woman with the weird haircut, had gotten the upper hand.

But staring at Shelly's terrified face, at her burgeoning belly, Chloe knew that this part of the day was lost.

But the battle was far from over.

Very, very far from being done.

"Good, now keep backing up," Bella ordered as she shuffled with Shelly out in front of her.

No matter what happened, Carson and Leland wouldn't do anything to Shelly, not with the precious cargo that she carried.

They still had five months to save them all.

To save everyone that was still living.

Chapter 53

A SHOT RANG OUT, and Robert instinctively ducked. Only it wasn't intended for him. In fact, he didn't think it was intended for anyone. It was a warning shot from Aiden.

He didn't want to shoot the kids.

Carson, on the other hand, strode forward as if nothing had happened, the children from both their pasts filing in behind him.

"Have you ever thought about it, Robert? About what decision you would make on the shores of the Marrow?"

Robert moved toward Carson.

"What happened to you, Carson? What happened that changed everything about who you are?"

Carson threw his head back and laughed.

"Ah the irony! What happened to me? What happened to *me*? Isn't that the question, hmm? What makes me *me*? What makes an individual unique?" He leaned in close, until their faces were mere inches apart. "*That* is what matters. That is the only thing that matters."

Helen, are you—?

But his thought was stolen from him when someone shambled into the room.

Robert pulled away, instinctively moving his arms behind him, doing his best to protect the humans at his back.

Carson also retreated, although not as violently as Robert had.

A man shambled into the room. An old man, hunched, withered, barely able to hold himself upright. At first, Robert thought that it was the Cloak.

And then the man raised his head, and Robert recognized the pale blue eyes, the line of a mouth, even though it was much older than he remembered.

It was Sean Sommers.

Recognition crossed Carson's face as well, and Robert suddenly realized what was about to happen.

"No!" he screamed, taking a step forward, but someone grabbed his arm. He tried to shrug the hand away, but it was too strong. "No!"

Carson strode toward Sean, who looked like he was having a hard time breathing, let alone walking. And then the students, the quiddity of the dead Guardians, moved with him.

As Robert watched, helpless to do anything, the kids, his friends, started to hold hands, forming a single-file line.

Sean didn't know what was happening, that much was clear. His eyes were completely white, his arms slack. Even when the closest child reached for his hand, Sean seemed oblivious. If anything, he almost seemed to grab it. At the same time, Carson went to his other side, and he too squeezed Sean's hand.

"No!" Robert again tried to pull away, but now there wasn't just one person holding him, but three.

"Robert, it has started. You can't stop it now."

It was a gravelly voice, the voice of the Cloak. He didn't turn to look at him.

Instead, his eyes were locked on the scene before him, reminiscent of his time at Seaforth.

"Yes! Yes!" Carson screamed. "It's happening! Daddy's coming home!"

Sean's body seemed to stretch like warm taffy, and the clouds above started to swirl again. In a matter of moments, the ceiling was gone, disappeared, and the clouds were back. Lightning illuminated the sky like Fourth of July fireworks.

And then, amidst the sound of children's laughter, Sean started to be pulled apart.

Light shot out of his ancient eyes, mouth, and nose.

But the largest beacon was from his chest, which spread wide.

Robert knew what was coming next. Carson had found his Guardian, and unlike at Seaforth when he had bound Father Callahan to the dead woman and his own living body, this time was different.

This time he had bound a Guardian to the dead, to quiddity of dead Guardians, and to himself, Carson, who was also a Guardian.

The rift opened much quicker than it had at Seaforth. Without the child, it couldn't be kept open, the two worlds would still remain separate, but Robert knew there was something different about this time. This time it might just remain open long enough for someone, or some*thing*, to come through.

And he wanted that one person to be Amy, *needed* it to be her.

He saw the waves inside the beach-ball-sized hole in Sean's chest first, and then he screamed when he saw the hat.

In addition to Leland, there were others on the shore, one of whom he recognized immediately.

"Amy!" he screamed, thrashing against the arms that held him with all their might. "Amy! Come out! Come through! *Come back to me!*"

There were two others on the beach: one was a guard from the prison and the other was Allan Knox. Robert stretched his hand out, tears streaming down his face.

"Come! Amy! *Amy!*"

Two hands gripped the sides of Sean's ribcage, but they weren't the small, delicate hands of an eight-year-old girl. They weren't Amy's hands.

They were weathered.

And then a wide-brimmed black hat peeked through.

"Robert, please! We have to go! I know a way out! Please, Robert! Come with us!"

Before he could respond, Leland pulled himself out of Sean's chest, and into the world of the living.

At first, Robert saw a massive, winged beast covered in thick, leathery scales, talons that reached high, nearly to the ceiling that no longer existed. A forked tongue, feet like hooves.

But then the beast shuddered and shrunk back into a human form. Slowly, almost mechanically, Leland raised his gaze.

And once again, it was Robert's face that he saw staring back at him.

Only his reflection was smiling, while Robert was weeping, crying for his daughter miles below in a land that he could never reach.

Epilogue

THIRTY-ONE YEARS AGO

"SEAN! GRAB THE BOYS! *Grab them!*"

Sean didn't need any clarification as to who of the nineteen children the woman was speaking of.

She wanted him to grab *her* boys.

Sean didn't hesitate. He ran into the room, encouraging all of the children to get up as he passed them.

"Get up! Come on, kids! We have to move, *now!*" Sean didn't know what he had to say to get them moving, but his current approach didn't seem to be working; the children seemed rooted in place.

There's no time for this.

"Robert! Get up!"

Sean knew that, unlike his brother, Robert hated to be singled out, and as predicted the boy's head was down when he got to his feet and didn't even see him.

"Come with me! Everyone follow me!" the woman cried from the door.

When Robert started to head in her direction, Sean grabbed him by the collar. Then he grabbed his brother with his other hand.

"No, not that way," Sean whispered. "We're going this way."

Robert finally raised his head to look at Sean. His eyes were wide, and he struggled against his grip on his shirt in silent protest.

"What about Mom?"

Sean turned his head to look at the woman. Chloe Black had initially been opposed to the idea of collecting all of the future Guardians in one central location, for fear that their concentrated meditations would alert Leland to their position. But she had eventually acquiesced, as it was the only thing that made logistical sense to Sean; at the rate that the other Guardians were being hunted down and killed, they didn't have much time—they needed to train the children as quickly as possible. But now, seeing Chloe standing by the doorway with her arms outstretched, sheltering them like some sort of mother hen, he knew that she had been right all along.

His plan had been too hurried, too risky.

Too dangerous.

They locked eyes for a moment, and he saw a deep sadness in those hazel pools.

He knew what she wanted him to do, and while Sean had planned for the possibility of Leland finding them, he had never expected it to happen. And her look told him it was time to enact the plan.

A plan that didn't involve Chloe. They both knew that this was probably the last time that she would ever see her boys alive.

A quick nod from the woman, and Sean turned, pulling her boys with him. While the other children went out the door that Sean had burst through, they went the other way.

At the back of the classroom was a utility closet, and Sean flung the door open and guided the boys inside. A glance over his shoulder revealed that the others had already fled the classroom. He hoped that they made it, that they escaped, but deep down he had his reservations.

Leland was a—

"Stop," he scolded himself. Robert looked up at him as he spoke, but Sean shook his head. "No, not you," he muttered.

The room was small for the three of them, and it was filled with supplies that looked to be straight out of an antique movie set. But the ladder was there where he had left it.

Wrapping his hands around the worn wood, he moved it to the center of the room. Testing it with his hands, hopeful that it would hold, he turned his gaze upward.

"Go on, Robert. You first."

"Go up?"

Sean nodded and pointed at the air vent in the center of the ceiling. Now it was Robert's turn to nod. Then the boy, as obedient as he was, started up the ladder, while Sean held the sides as it trembled under his weight.

Robert slid the vent cover to one side, just as Sean had instructed. The boy looked down at him then, and Sean felt what little patience he had left wane.

They were running low on time.

"Go, Robert! Just go!"

Robert frowned, then disappeared into the vent.

Sean turned to Carson next.

"Your turn," he said.

But unlike Robert, Carson was more inquisitive, less apt to simply follow directions without so much as an explanation. In fact, the only thing that he seemed to share with his brother was the same sad expression.

"Who are we running from?"

There was a high-pitched scream from somewhere in the hallway and Sean gritted his teeth.

"Hurry, Carson! Just *climb!*"

The boy hesitated, and for a brief, terrifying moment, Sean pictured him unwilling to move. And then he pictured him having to knock him out and carry his body up the ladder. To his surprise, however, the boy stepped to action, giving him a look as he placed a worn running shoe on the first rung, then the second.

Later, you will tell me everything later, the look said, which was fine by Sean.

If there was a later.

As the boy disappeared after his brother, Sean gave one final look at the classroom, and came to the sinking realization that Chloe had been right all along; it had been a mistake coming here. And whatever happened to those kids…that was on him.

Swallowing hard, he made his way up the teetering ladder and then squeezed himself into the duct.

It was dark and smelled of earth inside the aluminum tunnel, what with the ventilation system not having been used for at least a decade.

Or maybe two.

One of the first things that Sean had done when scouting this place had been to look for passages such as this one, to design escape routes, if needed.

There was only one: this one. This vent, for whatever reason, was just large enough for a full-grown man such as himself to squeeze through.

Which was what he did now.

"Keep moving forward," he instructed as loudly as he dared. "Move on your stomach…move as quietly as you can. In about fifty feet, you should see a hole going down. Stop in front of it and wait for me. Do you understand?"

"Yes," a meek voice replied. He didn't know which of the brothers it was who answered, but he didn't care, either.

"Then go," Sean encouraged.

Like some sort of human centipede, the three of them started to shuffle forward, their movements stirring up enough dirt and dust to coat the inside of Sean's throat.

Sean had only gone about fifteen feet when the real screaming started.

The sounds were muted in the ventilation system, and they had acquired a metallic-like quality to them, but they were still horrible.

There were few things in this world worse than a child's screams, and there was nothing worse than seventeen of them wailing all at once.

And they seemed to be coming from directly below them.

Sean bumped into Carson's feet, who had stopped moving. Heart racing, he gave the boy's sneaker a shove.

"Keep moving! We have to keep moving!" he hissed.

Words drifted up to him, breaking the monotony of the screams.

"Don't do this! Leland, don't you do this...these kids have done nothing. It's me you want. Take me, but let them go."

Sean heard Leland laugh.

"Let them go? Why would I let them go? Isn't their ultimate goal in life to sacrifice themselves? Isn't that what you're trying to teach them, anyway? To get them to believe that their uniqueness, their self, means nothing? That they should just give up who they are? Well, then, I'm just helping them on their way!"

"Leland! No!!!"

Even in the duct, Sean heard the undeniable sound of a blade slicing through fabric and the skin beneath.

A single tear made a track down Sean's dirt-smeared face.

He swore under his breath and shoved Carson's shoe again, but the boy resisted.

"Go!" he sobbed. "We. Have. To. Keep. *Moving.*"

Carson looked back at him, his eyes the only thing visible in the near blackness of the massive air vent.

"It's Robert, he stopped."

Sean ground his teeth in frustration, and was going to call out to the boy when Leland's voice filtered up at him again.

"Where are my boys? You can't keep them from me!"

"You will never find them, Leland. Never. You mark my—"

Chloe's words were cut short, punctuated by her own scream.

Then another.

And another.

"You gonna tell me where my boys are now? No?"

Another scream, this one followed by the sound of something wet sluicing onto the hard orphanage floor. Sean, fully crying now, wanted more than anything to be down there, to help her, to take out Leland.

But he had a job to do, a job whose singular focus was to protect these two boys.

He wouldn't let Chloe die in vain. It was the least he could do.

Sean grunted and started to crawl again, driving Carson forward with his weight. It made much more noise than he would have liked, but at least they had started to inch forward again.

Breathing heavily, the screams from below, as horrible as they were, thankfully masked what must have sounded like a toolbox bolus making its way through the intestines of an iron giant.

And then, when he arrived at the spot where Robert had stopped, he realized with horror why the boy had ceased crawling.

There was a grate on the floor of the vent, a window into the hallway below. And the scene it revealed was one of pure carnage.

All seventeen children were lying on the ground, their bodies twisted into some facsimile of the fetal position.

Their eyes were mostly open, as were their mouths. And they all lay in pools of their own blood.

And then there was Chloe, lying on her side, staring directly up at him.

Her face had been flayed like a country roast, her glistening flesh pulled down in strips like a carnivore cheese-string.

And Robert had seen all of this—his own mother, for Christ's sake. Even Sean, hardened as he was, felt his stomach lurch at the sight.

Staring down at Chloe's mangled face, he mouthed the words, *I promise*, and then he pushed onward.

***

The opening in the duct led to a furnace room, and Sean somehow managed to squeeze by the two boys and then descend into the depths. From there, he was able to help them down next.

He couldn't look them in the eyes anymore, particularly Robert, knowing what he had seen. Instead, he glanced about the room. The single lone bulb above them, paltry as it was, was so much brighter than the interior of the vent that he took a moment to orient himself.

There.

Sean moved to the far wall, conscious that he must hurry, that at any moment Leland could burst into the small eight-by-eight-foot furnace room and do to them as he had done to the others.

There was a large air filter resting against the wall, and he pulled it away, revealing a crudely carved out opening in the wall. Taking his lighter from his pocket, he held it into the opening, revealing a dirt tunnel that extended into darkness.

Only then did he turn back to the boys.

"Through here. I want you to go through here and run as fast as you can."

Robert's face was a shade of white that Sean had never seen on a living being before. For the second time in less than an hour, he thought he was going to have to brain one of the Black brothers and carry them with him. But the boy, as in shock as he was, did as he was ordered, cautiously entering the tunnel before breaking into a run. Carson followed quickly after Robert, giving Sean the same look as he had back in the storage room in the back of the classroom.

One day you are going to tell me everything.

And then Sean hurried after them.

He had gone maybe forty yards when he heard heavy breathing from behind him, and he whipped around. His hands groped for Robert and Carson behind him in an attempt to make sure that he protected them.

It's that bastard Leland, he somehow found us...after killing all the other kids, now he is coming for them.

But they had obeyed his instructions and had continued to run and his hands found air.

"Lela—" But he stopped speaking when he realized that it wasn't Leland.

It couldn't be Leland; the silhouette was too small to be Leland.

Sean pulled his lighter out again and flicked it on.

A little girl with big green eyes and blonde hair shielded her face from the light.

"What are you doing here?" he hissed, the words coming out more angrily than he had expected.

She shrugged, and wiped tears from her face.

"I followed you," she whimpered. "I saw...I saw..."

Sean held up a hand, stopping her mid-sentence as he mulled his options. Taking the girl with them would slow them down, reduce the chances of any of them getting out of here alive.

And as much as he felt for this little orphan girl, he had made a promise to Chloe—a promise to keep her sons safe, no matter what.

And it was a promise he intended on keeping.

Sean reached out and the girl recoiled. Frustrated, he stepped forward again and grabbed her by the collar.

"I'm sorry, Shelly," he said softly. Tears unexpectedly burst from her eyes. "I'm sorry that you had to see that," he sobbed, "no one should have seen that."

He pulled her on the other side of him, deeper in the tunnel, into the boys' wake.

He was going to keep his promise to Chloe; he would keep the boys alive. But he wasn't going to sacrifice this innocent girl in the process.

There had been enough death at Sacred Heart this day to last a lifetime.

As they moved deeper into the tunnel, the air got thinner, their breathing more laborious, and he started to think hard about where they were going to go should he manage to get out of here alive.

He had heard of a church, of a man who helped keep strays, with no questions asked. Somewhere far away.

A priest, one with a penchant for helping those in need.

He would go there, Sean decided at long last.

And when Robert and Carson Black were finally safe, he would be the one to do the tracking.

Leland would pay; the man was going to pay for what he had done here.

That was another promise that Sean Sommers was determined to keep.

END

Author's Note

The Haunted Series keeps growing in terms of its scope and the number of characters involved. I hope you enjoy the fact that I have brought in several characters from my *Family Values Trilogy*, and if you did, then you'll be happy to know that there just might be some guest appearances from my other series' as well.

SACRED HEART ORPHANAGE is the penultimate book in Season 1 of the Haunted Series. The next book, tentatively titled **'THE MARROW'** will be the *Season Finale*. This is by no means the end of the series, but represents an end to Robert's journey from an accountant to a Guardian responsible for the fate of the world. Season 2 will focus on the results of his decisions, both good and bad, and the way they shaped the world.

I also have plans to write other books related to *The Haunted Series*, including a prequel that delves deeper into Leland and Sean's relationship long before Robert was around. And then there's Allan and Ben... I could have just let Ben Tristen, Warden of Seaforth Prison, die, but I just like the guy too damn much. Both he and Allan still have a role to play in Robert and his World, but in the meantime, they also have their own adventures in the Marrow that I would love to share with you. There are backstories on the evil in *The Haunted Series* (Jonah, Michael, James Harlop, Carson himself) that might also be of interest. As always, I'm open to suggestions... I mean, I write my books for you guys, my readers, so if there is anything you guys are dying to know about, just drop me a line.

Too many stories, too little time, too much carpel tunnel.

I'll see you next month with Book 5 in *The Haunted Series*. In the meantime, grab a drink, a snack, and curl up with a good book.

And, as always, you can reach me by email (patrick@ptlbooks) or on my Facebook page (@authorpatricklogan).

You keep reading and I'll keep writing.

Patrick
February 2017, Montreal

62670496R00146

Made in the USA
Lexington, KY
14 April 2017